"I want you, Shannon."

Shannon stared, the significance of the words sinking in. "You don't mean..." Surely he wasn't suggesting what she thought he was.

Devin spoke in that same level, apparently reasonable tone. "I mean exactly what I said. Do you have a problem?"

It was a moment before her voice would work, and when it did it was higher and shriller than she intended it to be. "Damn right I have a problem! You can't ask me to agree to that!"

"I can ask you to do anything I please." He thrust both hands into his pockets and rocked back slightly on his heels, his eyes focused on her face. "I can't compel you to agree, of course. The choice is entirely yours."

Daphne Clair lives in subtropical New Zealand, with her Dutch-born husband. They have five children. At eight years old she embarked on her first novel, about taming a tiger. This epic never reached a publisher, but metamorphosed male tigers still prowl the pages of her romances. She has won literary prizes for short stories and non-fiction, and has also published poetry. As Laurey Bright she writes for Silhouette®. Daphne welcomes letters to Box 18240, Glen Innes, Auckland, Aotearoa/New Zealand.

Recent titles by the same author:

HIS TROPHY MISTRESS

THE MARRIAGE DEBT

BY
DAPHNE CLAIR

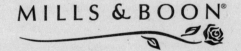

MILLS & BOON®

DID YOU PURCHASE THIS BOOK WITHOUT A COVER?

If you did, you should be aware it is **stolen property** as it was reported *unsold and destroyed* by a retailer. Neither the author nor the publisher has received any payment for this book.

All the characters in this book have no existence outside the imagination of the author, and have no relation whatsoever to anyone bearing the same name or names. They are not even distantly inspired by any individual known or unknown to the author, and all the incidents are pure invention.

All Rights Reserved including the right of reproduction in whole or in part in any form. This edition is published by arrangement with Harlequin Enterprises II B.V. The text of this publication or any part thereof may not be reproduced or transmitted in any form or by any means, electronic or mechanical, including photocopying, recording, storage in an information retrieval system, or otherwise, without the written permission of the publisher.

This book is sold subject to the condition that it shall not, by way of trade or otherwise, be lent, resold, hired out or otherwise circulated without the prior consent of the publisher in any form of binding or cover other than that in which it is published and without a similar condition including this condition being imposed on the subsequent purchaser.

MILLS & BOON and MILLS & BOON with the Rose Device are registered trademarks of the publisher.

First published in Great Britain 2002
Harlequin Mills & Boon Limited,
Eton House, 18-24 Paradise Road, Richmond, Surrey TW9 1SR

© Daphne Clair de Jong 2002

ISBN 0 263 82951 0

Set in Times Roman 10½ on 12½ pt.
01-0702-39142

Printed and bound in Spain
by Litografia Rosés, S.A., Barcelona

CHAPTER ONE

'DARLING Shannon! Congratulations. A great little film.'

Shannon Cleary turned from the group she was with to accept an enthusiastic kiss on her cheek. 'Thanks, Lloyd. I hope you'll say so in your review.' Half the country read his column.

'But of course, darling! I always said you're one of New Zealand's most promising young directors.' His eyes shifted to somewhere beyond her. 'Excuse me, there's someone I must see...' He patted her shoulder and disappeared into the crowd milling about the foyer of Auckland's trendiest cinema.

Shannon's escort, a hand at her waist, murmured in her ear, 'Pretentious little hypodermic.'

Shannon laughed, but the laughter snagged in her throat when a few yards away a dark masculine head turned at the sound, and gleaming obsidian eyes under thick black lashes and resolute brows caught her gaze and held it.

Her own eyes widened and her heart made a weird convolution. Everything seemed suddenly sharper, painfully clear and bright, as if she were looking through a lens being brought into perfect focus.

She was conscious of the babble of voices, of Craig

5

Sloane's protective arm at her back, of the gilt-framed mirrors on the foyer walls reflecting the colours of women's dresses, a flash of jewellery, and then a glimpse of her own face stark with shock—lips slightly parted, the green irises of her eyes almost obliterated by the darkened centres as she wrenched her gaze from the man who was looking at her with undiluted attention.

The reflection was blocked out as he moved toward her, and she concentrated on the immaculate white shirt he wore under a perfectly tailored jacket, until he stood in front of her and the well-remembered wine-dark voice said, 'Shannon…'

Somehow the other people around melted away, all except Craig. His hand tightened on her waist, and she was thankful because her knees were threatening to buckle.

Forcing her expression to a wooden indifference, Shannon dredged up her voice from where it had re-treated deep into her lungs. 'Devin. What are you do-ing here?'

His brows lifted a fraction. 'I came to see your film. Your first director's credit on a full-length feature, isn't it?'

'Yes.' Shannon's voice was stiff. 'I hope you en-joyed it.'

Straight black lashes flickered, his glance sharpen-ing as though looking for a hidden meaning. Then he seemed to relax, one hand in a pocket of his trousers. The sculpted mouth moved in the barest semblance of a smile. 'Very much.' He paused, moved his appraising gaze to Craig and said coolly, 'You were good too.' Craig had filled the lead male role as a young city man lost in the bush and discovering his own inner strengths and weaknesses.

'He did a superb job.' Glad of the excuse to look away from Devin, Shannon turned a warm smile on Craig. 'I'm lucky to have worked with him.'

Craig's answering white-toothed smile and sparkling blue eyes showed his elated mood. 'Thanks, hon.' He bent and kissed her mouth, a friendly peck. 'That's mutual.'

Devin's eyes had gone hard, with the glitter of polished steel. 'Aren't you going to introduce me?' he asked Shannon.

'Craig,' she said fatalistically, 'this is Devin.'

'Hi.' Craig held out his hand, and after a moment Devin took it in a firm grip.

'Devin Keynes,' he said.

'Keynes?' Craig looked tentatively impressed.

'Shannon's husband.' Devin threw a lightning glance at her.

'Ex-husband,' she immediately corrected.

Craig looked from her to Devin, obviously startled.

Devin ignored him. 'I don't recall getting a divorce.'

More sharply than she'd meant to, Shannon reminded him, 'We're not married anymore.'

'The law says we are.'

'That's easily fixed.' She wished she were tall enough not to have to look up to meet his eyes.

'Do you have plans to remarry?' he asked her, a deadly mockery lacing his voice.

Shannon hedged. 'That's not the point—'

A young woman with spiked flame-red hair and an assortment of rings decorating her ears, nose and eyebrows, bounced up, hugged Shannon and offered more congratulations. 'I heard you're doing a feature film of your own next?'

'I hope to.' She planned to produce and direct it herself, rather than waiting to be hired again by a bigger production company, but the financial backing she was negotiating had not so far materialised.

'Good for you. I could be available in about six weeks if you need a production manager.'

'Thanks,' Shannon said, 'I'll keep that in mind.'

Another woman appeared out of the crowd. Sleek, blond, her curvy figure encased in a sheath of shimmering silver. 'Dev?' She tucked a hand into Devin's arm. 'We're on our way. The Borlands have invited us to supper.' She gave Craig a dazzling smile and held out her free hand. 'I'm Rachelle Todd. I *loved* you in the film.'

Craig grinned at her and modestly ducked his streaked-blond head.

Rachelle looked inquiringly at Shannon, and Devin introduced them, this time confining himself to names only. Rachelle made a vaguely complimentary comment on her directing skill before urging Devin away to join their party.

'Ex-husband?' Craig queried.

'I don't talk about it,' Shannon said shortly. 'And I don't suppose he does either.' It was no real secret, but she'd continued to work under her own name during their marriage, and deliberately not trumpeted her connection with a much more prominent one. The fact that she'd briefly been a member of one of New Zealand's richest families wasn't widely known.

'Touchy subject?' Craig's hand squeezed her waist. 'Don't worry, I won't spread it about.'

More people approached them, and Shannon tried to forget the unexpected encounter.

The film was received with mild to almost extravagant praise for the most part, although some reviewers ignored it, and one was scathing about the acting, the direction and the script, throwing Shannon into deep depression for several hours. Then she dug out the positive reviews that had preceded it and cheered herself up by re-reading them.

But the day her last hope for financing her own project fell through, she wanted to curl up in a corner and cry.

Instead she phoned Craig. 'If you're offered that TV part you auditioned for,' she said, 'you'd better take it.'

'Someone else got it,' he told her. 'What's happened?'

'I'm not going to be able to make *A Matter of Honour*. At least not this year.'

'Why?'

'The money hasn't come through after all. And I was so sure they couldn't turn me down this time...'

Craig commiserated. 'So we're in the sugar pile.' He sighed. 'Tell you what, I'll come round to your place, we'll find a pub and drown our sorrows.'

In the event Craig did considerably more 'drowning' than Shannon, and leaned heavily on her shoulder as he escorted her somewhat unsteadily back to her tiny flat in the old inner-city suburb of Ponsonby.

Once there she tipped him onto the sofa in the living room where he fell instantly asleep, and Shannon took herself off to the bathroom and then bed.

In the morning she fed him toast and tea, sitting across the kitchen table from him as he squinted at her blearily.

'How come you don't look the way I feel?' he demanded.

Shannon laughed. 'I didn't drink as much as you.'

'We're in the wrong business, you know that?'

'You want to become a bank clerk?'

He cast her a look, not bothering to answer but going off on a tangent. 'Your husband—'

'Ex.'

'Your ex-husband,' Craig amended. 'Is he one of the Keyneses that own half the printing firms in the country?'

'His family does,' Shannon acknowledged. 'Devin

made his own fortune out of digitised printing presses and copiers.' His company sold them worldwide, and she knew he had interests in several other businesses.

'Ah—fortune. That's the operative word.' Craig wagged a finger at her.

'What?' Shannon stared at him, deliberately obtuse. 'If you're thinking—'

'I'm thinking that your husband—ex, whatever— might be a good bet for a backer.'

'Uh-uh.' Shannon shook her head.

'You seem to be on reasonable terms with him.'

'Brawling in public isn't Devin's style,' nor hers, 'but he wouldn't dream of investing in any project of mine.' She couldn't imagine why he'd turned up at the premiere. Unless the blond and beautiful Rachelle had dragged him along.

'Have you asked him?'

'Of course not! I know he'd say no.'

Craig leaned forward. 'Sometimes people surprise you. How long since you two separated?'

'Three years. Why?'

'People can change a lot in that time. I did hear that someone else is interested in the Duncan Hobbs trial.'

'Who?' Shannon demanded, dropping the knife she was using to butter toast. 'That's *my* story!'

'History is anybody's, Shan, you can't copyright it. Jack Peterson's supposed to be the director they have in mind.'

Peterson's name was enough to have producers and investors scrambling for a piece of the action. 'I don't have a hope now of getting funding this year, and by next year it could be too late, if someone else gets in first.'

'Why don't you ask your husband?' Craig urged. 'After all, who else do you know with that kind of money?'

No one, of course. She stared back at him helplessly.

He got up from the table. 'Do you have his number?'

Shannon shook her head. 'I haven't spoken to him for years—until the other night. What are you doing?'

He'd opened the telephone book on the shelf below the wall phone. 'Looking him up.'

'You're crazy.'

'Maybe.' Craig's roving finger stopped in the middle of a page. 'This should be him.'

'Craig!' She pushed back her chair and got up, but he was already dialling.

Even as she snatched the receiver from his hand she heard faintly from the other end a deep, unmistakable voice say, 'Keynes here.' And then, 'Hello?'

'Go on!' Craig took her hand and lifted it, pressing the receiver to her ear. 'Ask him.'

'Who is this?' Devin's voice was suddenly louder, imperative.

'It's me,' she said. 'Shannon.'

She thought he might have cut her off, the silence was so complete. 'Shannon?' he said at last. 'What the hell's going on?' Craig was still close, trying to hear, only inches from her.

She grimaced at him. 'Nothing.' Craig made a fearsome face and growled in his throat.

Shannon couldn't help laughing, a small, smothered sound. He mouthed *'Go on!'* at her.

'Um,' she said into the phone, 'I wondered if I could ask you something.'

'Ask me what?'

When she didn't immediately answer, her mind scrabbling for sensible words while instinct told her to hang up, Devin said impatiently, 'I'm on my way to the airport. If this is important—'

'No,' she said hastily. 'I mean, it's very important to me, but if it's a bad time…' Blurting out the request wouldn't do. He'd simply say no and that would be that. If she could only make him listen to her proposal there might be a slim chance of persuading him.

As she hesitated he said harshly, 'I have better things to do than join in your games, Shannon.'

'It isn't a game!' Did he think this was fun for her? 'Maybe we could talk sometime?' she suggested hurriedly. 'After you get back from wherever you're going?'

The line was silent again for a few seconds before he said, 'Your timing was never all that good. I'll be back tomorrow.' He paused again. 'We could have dinner if you like.'

'Oh, I…th-thank you.'

Craig hissed, 'What's he saying?'

She covered the mouthpiece. 'He's inviting me to have dinner with him.' Removing her hand, she tried to ignore Craig's frantically nodding head.

Devin sounded markedly cool, but he was saying, 'I'll get my secretary to book us a table and I'll pick you up around seven-thirty.' He paused a moment, then rattled off her address as if he knew it by heart, 'Is that right?'

'Yes,' she said, mechanically.

'Now excuse me, or I'll miss my flight.'

Shannon put the phone down in a daze. 'I'm seeing him tomorrow night,' she said.

'Great!' Craig grabbed her and planted a light kiss on her lips.

'He'll probably laugh in my face, and I don't know why I let you talk me into this.'

'Because of my fatal charm!' He grinned at her. 'Come on, hon. You never know, he might just say yes after all. And at least you'll get a decent meal out of it.'

She got rid of Craig as soon as she could, then returned to the phone and began calling up contacts.

There were indeed rumours that another production team was sniffing about what she'd come to consider her story. By the time she prepared to meet Devin she was nervous and increasingly determined to give this idea, mad though it might be, her best shot.

After discarding three possible outfits she settled on faux silk pearl-grey pants and a black satin top with a short beaded jacket over it. Releasing her thick brown hair from its practical tied-back style, she brushed it to a sheen and let it wave about her shoulders.

When the doorbell rang she opened the door to Devin, a black satin bag clutched in her hand.

'We have plenty of time,' he told her. 'Are you going to invite me in?'

Shannon stepped back reluctantly and he joined her in the narrow hallway, looking down at her for a second. His eyes took in the discreet make-up on her eyes and lips, and slipped over the rest of her. 'Very nice,' he said.

'Thank you.' She gestured at the darkened doorway behind him, and switched on the light.

He stopped in the centre of the Belgian rug, looking round with critical eyes.

Shannon had set the overstuffed pumpkin-coloured sofa against a cream wall that held a collection of funky little mirrors she'd picked up in second-hand shops and hung in a random pattern, each reflecting a tiny piece of the room. One deep armchair was covered in ruby-red fabric, the other in dark forest green. Scatter cushions on the chairs echoed the colours of the patterned rug and gave a touch of luxury.

Devin strolled to a set of shelves and picked up a Venetian glass rooster with an extravagant plumed tail of gold, green and blue tail feathers, and an erect red comb that matched the ruby chair. His hands followed the fluid contours of the glass. 'You still have it.'

He had given it to her on their honeymoon, when

she'd taken a fancy to it in an art shop. 'I still like it,' she said. 'And it goes with the room.'

She recalled picking it up on some confused impulse and putting it with some clothes and books when she'd packed up her things, severed her relationship with Devin. Pulling it out later when she'd furnished her new home she'd wanted to weep, and debated hiding it away. But in some obscure way it had been a comfort during a bleak, lonely time, a tenuous link with a happier past.

Replacing the rooster, Devin turned and surveyed the small room again. His gaze lingered on a large abstract painting, inspecting the vibrant primary colours splashed on the canvas in bold strokes. He moved closer to read the artist's name. 'Expensive, isn't he?' he queried. 'Though I could never see quite why.'

'He gave me a special price.' She had met the painter at a party in his studio that a friend took her along to, and had bought the painting on sight. She wasn't surprised that Devin didn't appreciate her taste. 'Do you want a drink?'

'No, thanks. I'll have some wine at dinner.'

'Well then…shall we go?' He made her nervous, prowling around her home.

She switched off the living room light and he opened the front door for her. 'Shall I turn off this light?' he asked, his hand on the hall switch as she passed him in the doorway.

'No.' Descending the steps she said, 'I leave it on

when I'm out so I don't come home to a darkened place.'

'You live alone?' He went ahead of her on the path and opened the door of his car, maroon and low-slung but roomy.

'Yes,' she said, sliding into the passenger seat.

Devin closed the door and came round to the other side. His sleeve brushed against her arm as he fastened his safety belt, and she felt a disconcerting frisson of awareness before he inserted the key in the ignition and the engine purred into life. 'So who was with you yesterday morning?' he asked as the car picked up speed.

'You...knew there was someone?'

'It was rather obvious.' His voice was bleak and desert-dry.

She slanted a look at him, but the dim light fleetingly thrown by a street lamp didn't help to define his expression, which was seldom simple to assess anyway. 'It was Craig. Craig Sloane.'

For a few moments he drove in silence. Then, in a curiously detached tone, he said, 'So you're sleeping with your handsome leading man.'

'I'm not sleeping with him!' Before she could stop herself, she shot at him, 'Are you sleeping with the divine Rachelle?'

He looked at her, then laughed as he returned his gaze to the road and the traffic. 'Do you care?'

'Of course not.' A lie, she dismayingly discovered, almost suffocating with unreasoning jealousy.

Stupid, she told herself. For three years she'd managed to blot any thought of Devin with another woman out of her mind, tell herself it no longer concerned her.

Which it didn't.

'If you're not lovers,' he said, 'what was Craig doing at your place?'

'He used my sofa. He was a bit…under the weather.'

'Drunk.'

'Tipsy.'

'Like I said.'

Shannon compressed her lips.

Devin swung the car around a corner. 'And if he hadn't been…'

Shannon shrugged. She didn't need to justify herself to him, and objected to being cross-questioned.

Devin persisted. 'Are you telling me you haven't let him into your bed yet?'

'I'm not telling you anything,' she snapped. 'My love life is none of your business.'

'We're married,' he reminded her.

'We are not married! We haven't been for the last three years.'

'Your choice.'

'You forced me to choose!'

'Is that how you see it?' His scorn was patent.

'There's no point in going over all that again.'

He stopped for a traffic light and turned to look at her. 'You're right. Let's leave the past where it is and move to the present. Does Craig know you're out with me tonight?'

'It was his idea.'

'*His* idea?'

'To phone you. I told him it wouldn't do any good.'

'You've lost me. Any good for whom?'

'Can't this wait until dinner?' she asked. After all, the whole idea of having a meal together was so that they could talk, wasn't it? In the comfort of a restaurant, with a good meal hopefully making him amenable to her request.

Someone tooted impatiently. The light had turned green.

'Okay,' Devin said on a tight, irritated note. Shannon wasn't sure if he was addressing her or the aggressive driver behind them. He released the brake and the car glided forward.

After a while she asked, 'How did you know where I live?'

'It's not a secret, is it? You're in the phone book.'

'No, it's not a secret.'

'Well, then…' He shrugged as if the subject bored him, and for the rest of the journey into the central city he concentrated on his driving.

It wasn't until they had ordered from the glossy menu in the expensive restaurant he'd chosen—or that his secretary had chosen for him—that he leaned his forearms on the linen tablecloth, looked across the wreath of flowers surrounding a squat gold candle in a glass bowl, and said, 'So why did you phone me,

Shannon? If not just to give your bedmate a bit of kinky titillation?'

Shannon clenched her fingers about her fork. 'Craig is not my bedmate. And if he were, I wouldn't have done a thing like that.'

Looking at her thoughtfully, he said, 'No, I don't suppose you would. Considering the company you keep you're surprisingly straitlaced in some ways.'

'Is that a complaint?' she asked, stung. Had he found her a boring lover? 'I'm sorry if I wasn't up to your expectations.'

'You know I had no complaints,' he said. 'I've never enjoyed such a…satisfactory relationship, as far as sex goes.'

'Satisfactory,' she repeated. 'Oh, thank you.'

'I've offended you,' he said calmly, but there was a lurking amusement in his eyes. 'You were all I had imagined, and more,' he said. 'You have a beautiful body that I still dream about, and you made love like an angel—a surprisingly shy and yet intriguingly sexy angel.'

'Angels have no sex,' Shannon rejoined. 'They're gender neutral.'

'Let's not be too literal.' He paused before saying with unusual deliberation, his lowered voice sending an insidiously pleasurable sensation curling down her spine, 'It was a transcendental spiritual experience making love with you, as well as a very pleasurable physical one.'

Transcendental? An extravagant word, especially

from Devin. But one that just about described it, for her as well as for him.

Not transcendental enough to keep them together. Her heart seemed to swell under the influence of something painful pushing against its walls from the inside. 'That's very…flattering,' she said, 'but I'm sure you've had equally *spiritual* experiences with other women.'

His face became mask-like. 'Cynicism is new for you,' he said.

'A pity I didn't have it when we met.' It might have helped armour her against what was to come.

For a split second she saw a blaze of anger in his eyes, and then the waiter brought wine and made a ritual of pouring, and by the time he'd gone Devin had assumed a bland expression that told her nothing about his feelings.

He lifted his glass to her silently and waited for her to raise hers before he drank.

Replacing his glass on the table, he asked, 'Do you want to know about Rachelle?'

'No.'

'We find each other useful for social occasions,' he said, ignoring her denial. 'We're not emotionally involved. She has a bad marriage behind her and isn't interested in an intimate relationship.'

So was he patiently waiting for her to become interested? And if they weren't emotionally involved, did that necessarily mean they weren't having sex? Some people were able to separate the two.

Don't go there. 'I'm not interested in your… girlfriends,' she told him.

'Sure?' His gaze searched her face.

'Absolutely. This meeting isn't about personal matters, Devin. I have a business proposition for you.'

'Business?' He leaned back in his chair, regarding her dispassionately.

It crossed her mind that if she'd worn something low-cut, clinging, seductive, she might have had a better chance at persuading him.

Immediately she dismissed the thought. As she'd just said, this was business, and seduction had no place in it.

'So,' he said, looking like a large, watchful animal, his eyes lynx-like and unblinking. 'What do you want from me, Shannon?'

She breathed deeply, quickly, and passed her tongue briefly over her lips. 'I need money,' she said. Might as well spit it out and get it over with. 'And I need it fast. You're the only person I know who has the kind of money I'm looking for.'

CHAPTER TWO

'I SEE.' Devin straightened, and folded his arms, his face showing only guarded curiosity. 'What is it? You've overspent and need a loan?'

'Nothing like that. I have a proposition for you.'

His brows rose. 'A proposition?'

'A business proposal.' She had to put a positive spin on this, convince him that he wouldn't be throwing cash down the drain. Devin was as hard-headed about money as any other successful businessman, probably more than most. 'It's an investment opportunity.'

'A film,' he guessed, his resigned, slightly contemptuous tone implying that he didn't think much of the idea. His eyes strayed to a neighbouring table where a party of a half dozen women were chattering and laughing.

Shannon leaned forward to catch his attention, trying to infuse all her passionate belief in the project into her voice, her eyes. 'A special film. It could be a *great* film if I can raise the finance. An international success.'

Devin still looked sceptical.

'New Zealand is hot at the box office right now,' Shannon pressed.

'Right up there with Hollywood?' Devin queried dryly.

Brushing aside the sarcasm, Shannon launched into her carefully prepared background pitch about the growing worldwide film market.

The party at the next table had ordered several bottles of wine and were obviously celebrating something. Shannon had to raise her voice a little.

The waiter brought their meals and Shannon picked up her knife and fork, but kept talking. She had hardly touched the tender pork medallions in their golden apricot and orange sauce when Devin, halfway through his medium-rare pepper steak, raised a hand. 'Eat your dinner,' he ordered. 'It's a shame to let it spoil.'

Maybe she'd said too much. Devin liked good food and good wine and enjoyed savouring it. She should have remembered that. In business she knew he was incisive, practical, getting straight to the point, known as a fast worker. But paradoxically he took his pleasures in more leisurely fashion, giving time to appreciating scents, tastes, textures.

He had made love like that, as if there was all the time in the world to explore the soft inner skin of her elbow with a fingertip, tracing the faint path of a blue vein, to sift his fingers through her hair and admire the silky fan of it falling against the pillow, to inhale the perfume she'd dabbed behind her ear, his tongue finding the shallow groove, and to delight in looking at her naked body, his head propped on one hand while the other made tantalising patterns about her breasts, her navel, touching lightly, teasing until she raised her arms and pulled him fiercely to her, unable to bear the exquisite torment any longer.

'What are you thinking about?'

His voice brought her back with a jerk to their surroundings. She realised she was sitting with her fork in her hand and probably a dreamy expression on her face. Hastily she lifted a piece of pork to her mouth, ducking her head as she cut another tender slice. 'This sauce,' she said. 'It's delicious.'

She must stop thinking that way, stop remembering. Their marriage was history now and they'd both come a long way.

She'd heard that Devin was spending a lot of time in America, after setting up a branch of his company there. After their split she'd consciously avoided places where she might expect to meet him, although she couldn't escape the odd news item, the unexpected encounter with a photograph in some magazine picked up in a doctor's waiting room, or an article about his company on the business pages of the daily paper.

She had hoped that when they did meet face to face she'd be able to confront him with indifference, their shared past a distant memory.

But one look at him and it had all come flooding back. The almost instant attraction of their first meeting, the golden-hazed weeks of his whirlwind courtship, their wedding day when the world was full of dazzling promise and they were certain their love would last forever and a day, despite the scarcely hidden dismay of his parents and family. The incredible pleasure of their lovemaking, and the way they'd seemed to be two halves of a whole, neither of them complete without the other.

And then the gradual disillusion and the pain of parting.

'Dessert?' Devin offered when she pushed away her plate.

Shannon shook her head, dispersing the memories. 'Maybe some cheese.'

A burst of laughter from their neighbours drowned her voice and Devin frowned. 'What?'

'I'll have the cheese board.' Shannon didn't share his surprising sweet tooth, but if he wanted something more she needed to be occupied rather than waiting for him to finish.

Devin ordered a chocolate mousse cake that came garnished with a generous swirl of whipped cream. He cut off a slice with a fork and offered it to Shannon.

Before she'd thought, she opened her mouth and allowed the morsel to slide onto her tongue. The achingly familiar, intimate gesture brought an unexpected sensation of tearing grief and regret. Appalled, she quickly swallowed the melting mouthful and grabbed at her wineglass, downing a gulp of red dessert wine to steady herself.

'Don't you like the cake?' he asked her.

'It's fine,' she answered huskily. 'Very…rich.'

He took a piece himself, half closing his eyes as he savoured it. 'Mmm,' he murmured. 'Superb.'

Shannon nibbled at bits of cheese while Devin finished the dessert. When he was done she pushed the board to him. 'Help yourself.'

He had a sliver of New Zealand-made Edam and a small piece of Gruyère, then said, 'Coffee?' And as the hilarity at the next table reached a new pitch, 'Or we could go back to my place and have it there.'

'Your place?'

'It's not far.' Watching her hesitate, he said with a touch of impatience, 'You know me better than to imagine I'm luring you into my lair for nefarious purposes. And it's a quieter place to talk than this.'

She had to agree with that. 'I could give you coffee at my place,' she offered reluctantly.

'Mine's closer. I'll see you home later.'

Maybe he'd feel more kindly disposed to her plans if she fell in with his suggestion. Though why he'd made it she wasn't sure. 'All right,' she said. 'If that's what you'd prefer.' He looked amused at her acquiescence, and she wondered if he was bending her to his will simply because he could, knowing she wanted something from him. Devin liked to be in control of any situation.

After settling the bill he ushered her back to his car, and within five minutes he was driving into an underground garage below one of the city's newer luxury residential buildings.

His apartment was on the fifth floor, and he guided

her into a large room with a picture window giving a view of the Waitemata Harbour at night, all winking city lights reflected like shot satin in the dark water.

Shannon's high heels sank into a slate-grey carpet, and Devin seated her on a deep couch covered in burgundy leather. Another couch and two matching burgundy chairs flanked a thick glass coffee table supported by hoops of burnished metal, and holding a striking bronze sculpture of an eagle with outspread wings.

'I'll get the coffee,' Devin said, walking to a wide doorway through which she glimpsed pale grey tiles and a granite counter.

A functional kitchen, she guessed, designed for efficiency. There would be no hanging bunches of dried herbs, or potted fresh ones on the windowsill, no antique utensils decorating the walls, as there had been in the cramped cottage she'd fallen in love with when they'd been inspecting the brand-new, soulless new town house for sale next door.

After noticing her yearning across the fence at the colonial relic with the overgrown lawn and neglected shrubs, Devin had made the owners an offer they couldn't refuse. An army of workers repaired the rusty guttering and worn boards, and modernised the kitchen and bathroom while Shannon had enlisted the help of an art director friend to bring the other rooms back to their quaint glory.

The place hadn't been at all suitable for Devin's lifestyle. Dinner parties had been necessarily small and intimate, and most of his business entertaining was conducted in restaurants, his office building or hired spaces.

After the break-up he'd lost no time, she guessed, in moving into this place.

Pale green walls showed off a couple of striking black-and-white photographs and a superrealist painting of a stream bed, every rounded rock and ripple in the water rendered with breathtaking precision, creating an irresistible urge to touch and check that it was only paint. Open glass doors led from the living room to a spacious formal dining room with a long table and high-backed chairs.

Everything looked elegant, expensive and impersonal.

Shannon ran her hand along a couple of rows of books on long shelves, finding biographies, history and true crime stories, a number of tomes dealing with economics and business practice, a pile of *National Geographic*s and a few other magazines. She was back on the couch, leafing through the latest issue of *Time,* when Devin returned with two bulbous ceramic mugs and sank down beside her, handing her one.

'Okay,' he said. 'Tell me what the film is about.'

She picked up her coffee, instinctively curving her palm about the warm, smooth shape of the mug. 'Have you heard of the Duncan Hobbs trial,' she asked, 'here in Auckland in 1898?'

'Should I have?'

'It was briefly mentioned in a TV programme last year.'

He shook his head. 'What did Duncan Hobbs do?'

'He was supposed to have raped the sister of his best friend's fiancée. The trial hinged on the evidence of his friend, the future brother-in-law of the victim.'

'Was he an eye-witness?'

'No, the evidence was mostly circumstantial. And not very consistent.'

'So, is this a whodunit?'

'A sort of did-he-do-it, anyway. But the point I'm more interested in is the personal dynamics—the change in the relationship between the engaged couple, the two sisters, and most of all the accused and his friend who was called on to testify…the choice he had to make as the key witness.'

Devin looked thoughtful. 'Support his best friend, and maybe alienate his bride-to-be…?'

'Exactly. It's a fascinating, true mystery story, and great for film. But expensive—the historical costumes and props, and even finding and adapting the settings, all add to the costs.'

'Couldn't you update it?'

Shannon shook her head. 'Attitudes have changed since then. They didn't even have women on juries, and a rape victim was often blamed for being in the wrong place at the wrong time, or for leading a man on. There are all sorts of reasons why it wouldn't work transferred to the twenty-first century.'

Devin leaned back a little. 'You seem to be in a hurry. It's not as though the story is topical.'

'I have a draft script, most of my crew almost ready to go, and I thought I had backing in the bag, but at the last minute I missed out after all.'

'How much do you need?'

When she told him, he didn't blink or move, but it was a second or two before he spoke. 'That's a lot of money.'

It was an enormous amount to her, but he was accustomed to dealing with sums that sported mind-boggling numbers of noughts. 'I don't know where else I could find the finance at short notice. And it's not actually a huge budget for a film.' She rushed on in the face of his stony silence. 'It isn't a big story with a cast of thousands and lots of special effects, but it could be an award winner, and do well overseas. The thing is, if we don't go into production soon the people I've lined up will have to take other work. Even Craig—'

'Craig?' A frown raked between his brows.

'I want him to play the witness.' And he wanted the part too. She was under no illusion that it was for her sake alone he'd pushed her into contacting Devin. She pulled several folded pages from her bag. 'I know most of the names won't mean much to you, but this is a short description of the project, with a list of potential cast and crew members and their credits. If you need me to explain anything…'

Devin nodded, and skimmed the pages while she watched, holding her breath.

Finally he looked up at her. 'I take it you've explored every other avenue before coming to me.'

'Everyone and anybody I could think of.'

'You went to people who know about the film business and they all turned you down.'

Shannon said frankly, 'I guess they weren't willing to invest that kind of money in a director with only one feature credit to my name. But I've lots of experience with my own short films and several assistant director credits. If they'd give me the chance I can do this. Or if you would…'

'A chance to the tune of millions of dollars.'

'It's a drop in the bucket to you!'

Devin laughed. 'Quite a few drops, in fact.' He stood up, strolled across the carpet and back, stopping within a few feet of her, regarding her with a disconcerting stare as if he wanted to see into her mind, her heart. 'This really matters to you.'

'I know you never thought much of my career, but it means a lot to me—'

'That I do know,' he said, 'since it's the reason you left me.'

'Not the only reason.' But she didn't want to get into that argument. There were dangerous waters there with hidden shoals. 'The thing is, will you help or am I wasting my time?'

'That depends,' he said, regarding her almost absently for a few seconds. A silky, ominous note in his voice, he said, 'What are you offering me in return?'

A tremor ran through her. Warning bells were ringing somewhere deep inside her mind. 'If it's a success you could make a pretty good profit.'

'A big if.'

Shannon couldn't dispute that. But she guessed Devin would make certain that if anyone gained financially from the venture, he did.

She tilted her head at a defiant angle. 'I can do it,' she reiterated, trying to infuse all her certainty into the words.

'You have great faith in yourself.'

'Yes,' she said. 'I do.'

Something complicated flickered across his face. 'I remember those words,' he said softly. 'But it didn't take you long to forget them.'

For a moment she was lost. Then she flushed. 'That isn't true! And it has nothing to do with this. We're talking about a deal here, a business deal.'

'You wouldn't have come to me if we hadn't had a personal relationship.'

She said fervently, 'Believe me, if I'd known anyone else who could afford to help me I'd have gone to them first.'

A gleam entered the dark eyes. 'So I'm a last resort.'

Had she offended him? Bad tactics. Trying to sound humble, she said, 'Put that way, it sounds like an insult. I didn't mean it to be. I just don't like asking favours…of anyone.'

'Especially me.' His face as usual revealed little of what he was thinking.

'I know we parted in anger, but after three years surely we can behave like civilised adults.'

Devin smiled, a slight, contained movement of his beautiful masculine mouth. 'If you can, I can.'

'Then will you think about this?' Shannon hoped she didn't sound as if she were begging. Trying for a more businesslike manner, she offered, 'I can draw up a formal proposal if you like, draft a contract.'

'I'd prefer my own lawyer to do that, I think.'

'Then you *will* think about it?' What the hell if she *was* begging? She would get down on her knees if necessary.

'I don't suppose you have any collateral to offer,' he asked, 'or guarantees?'

Shannon chewed on her lower lip. 'No. I have a car, but my flat's rented. I spent everything I had getting the script pulled together and hustling for grants or commercial backing.'

'I see.' He was looking at her in a speculative way that made her uneasy. Maybe he enjoyed watching her squirm.

'Look,' she said, 'if you're stringing me along I wish you'd just tell me it's no go. I'll find someone else…somehow.'

'Don't be so hasty. I haven't said no.'

'But you're not saying yes!'

'I need a little time to consider your…proposition. And maybe,' he added slowly, 'I have one of my own.'

'What do you mean by that?'

'How badly do you want this money?'

'You know I'm desperate. You said so yourself.'

He seemed to be looking through her rather than at her. She wished she knew what he was thinking, but Devin had never been easy to read. His emotions were hidden behind his classic, slightly austere features.

At last he spoke. 'I'll give you the money, but there's a condition.'

About to say, *Anything!* Shannon curbed the rash impulse. 'As long as it's not creative control over the project I can probably meet it.'

'Oh, you can meet it all right. All you need to do is say yes.'

'Yes to what? If you want your name in the credits I can bill you as co-producer if you like.'

A strange, unsettling smile lurked on his mouth. 'Not that.'

Shannon shook her head. 'Then what do you want?'

For a second or so he kept her on tenterhooks. Then he said, without any change in inflection, 'I want you, Shannon.'

CHAPTER THREE

SHANNON stared, the significance of the words sinking in. 'You don't mean…'

Surely he wasn't suggesting what she thought he was.

Devin said, in that same level, apparently reasonable tone, 'I mean exactly what I said. Do you have a problem?'

It was a moment before her voice would work, and when it did it was higher and shriller than she'd intended it to be.

'Damn right I have a problem! You can't ask me to agree to that!'

'I can *ask* you to do anything I please.' He thrust both hands into his pockets and rocked back slightly on his heels, his eyes focused on her face. 'I can't compel you to agree, of course. The choice is entirely yours.'

She stood up, her knees shaking. 'If this is a joke, you know what you can do with it.'

'You surely know me better than that.'

She gathered up her bag, straightened and stared at him with angry, indignant eyes. 'You can't possibly expect me to treat this seriously.'

Devin shrugged. 'Take it or leave it.'

36

Of course she couldn't take it. Nobody in their right mind would accept such a barbarous bargain. 'You know I won't!' she snapped.

'What's to stop you?' His voice turning low and coaxing, he said, 'I've missed you, Shannon. I've missed…this.'

He reached for her, in almost leisurely fashion, and to her later shame and despair she scarcely resisted when he drew her into his arms. One hand still clutching her purse, she instinctively raised her arms, checking herself before they went around him.

But when his mouth found hers, with a remembered confident persuasion, her heart tumbled over, and within moments her lips opened beneath his.

It was a kiss of surprising gentleness, seductive and slow but very thorough. Her eyes fluttered closed, the dancing harbour lights seeming imprinted on her lids, and she could have sworn the room was revolving in a sensuous waltz.

When Devin relinquished her mouth and she opened her eyes in a dazed stare, she saw him looking back at her with a questioning and grave expression. His eyes glittered and there was colour in his lean cheeks, the underlying bones appearing more prominent. 'Looks like I'm not the only one.'

He brought his mouth down again to hers, but this time she pushed against him, trying to break free, very nearly in a panic.

Although he didn't release his hold, his mouth lifted, his eyes burning. 'You don't hate me,' he said, his voice like heated black satin. She could almost feel it brush over her skin—they were so close that his breath touched her still parted lips.

She whispered, her shocked eyes held by his mesmerising gaze, 'I never said I hated you.'

She pulled away from him, trying to maintain some equilibrium. Devin let his hands drop from her waist, brushing over her hips before he let her go. 'Would it be so hard to accept my condition?'

'You really do mean it,' she said in disbelief. 'You're offering me money in return for…for—'

'For being with me again. It wouldn't be too much of a hardship, would it?' His expression was curiously watchful. 'Why don't you stay tonight?'

She moistened her lips. 'You make it sound so easy.'

Devin inclined his head. 'It's very simple. You say yes, we…go to bed, make love. Just like old times.'

'And tomorrow,' she queried, her throat raw, 'you'd give me a cheque? Payment for sex?'

He blinked, as if she'd shocked him. His eyes narrowed. 'For one night? Your price is too high.'

'One night or many, it makes no difference,' she pointed out, her voice shaking. 'Your…condition is unacceptable.'

'You've misunderstood me.'

'How?' she demanded. He'd been pretty explicit, she thought.

'I want more than sex. More than one night. I want you back in my life, Shannon. In my home. My bed.'

'Why?'

Devin looked down for a moment as if she'd caught him unawares with the question. 'Why?' he repeated. Then, slowly, 'Call it…a trial reconciliation.'

She looked around the coldly glossy designer-created apartment he called home now. He couldn't be serious. Despite the devastatingly sexy kiss she couldn't help suspecting some other motive than a sudden overwhelming desire to attempt a renewed relationship.

'A trial?' she repeated. 'For how long?'

'As long it takes…'

'To make the film? It could be five or six months!' She knew she sounded appalled.

A shadow of annoyance showed in his eyes. 'That's the deal,' he said curtly. 'Don't pretend it would be so enormous a sacrifice.' Arrogantly he added, 'You still want me.'

She could hardly deny that. Not after the way she'd succumbed to his kiss.

'You know I want your money,' she said, fighting for some sort of equilibrium. 'And you're saying you'd be willing to give it to me if I agree to…sell myself to you?' Her whole being revolted at the idea, and she had to question his motive. He'd had three years to suggest a revival of their marriage without resorting to a kind of extortion that was guaranteed to arouse her hostility.

'You're making it sound sordid,' he said shortly.

'You were the one who did that!' she said with

scorn. 'I just want to make sure we both know what the *terms* are.' Surely he could see that his blatant attempt at manipulation could only backfire—if he was genuinely interested in a reconciliation. 'I assume,' she said, in an attempt to make him see the enormity of his suggestion, 'you'd have it written into the contract and signed by witnesses?'

He said stiffly, 'This would be a private arrangement. Between the two of us.'

'I don't suppose it would stand up in court anyway.'

She shouldn't even be discussing it. 'I'd like to go home now,' she said. 'Maybe you could call me a taxi.'

'I'll take you.' His tone was brusque and he didn't move immediately, but when she turned toward the door he followed and opened it for her, blocking her way. 'By the way,' he said, 'what happened to Duncan Hobbs?'

'He was found guilty, though there was considerable public outrage about the verdict.'

'So what do you think? Was he guilty?'

'I don't know. There are some strange gaps in the prosecution case.'

He nodded slightly, then stepped back, and as she passed him he said, 'Think about my offer. You can phone me at the office during the day, or here anytime. If I'm not around leave a message and I'll get back to you.'

They rode to her flat in silence and she bade him an almost inaudible goodnight, slipping into the lighted hallway and leaning against the closed door as she heard his footsteps recede down the short pathway and then the faint sound of his car driving away.

She could still feel Devin's kiss on her lips, and his masculine scent was in her nostrils, lingering.

Imagination, she told herself, and walked to the bathroom, switched on the light and saw herself in the mirror over the basin. Her cheeks were delicately flushed, her eyes lustrous and the pupils large, dark, mysterious. Her mouth had lost the pink gloss she'd smoothed on before leaving, but her lips were red and full. She looked like a woman who had just left her lover.

Closing her eyes, she doused her face with cold water. How could he make her look like that with a single kiss? How could he make her heart beat faster, her blood run hot and swift in her veins, her whole being flood with longing?

She had got over the break-up of her marriage, gone on with her life, closed off the memories, except for those that surfaced in unguarded sleep.

The whole thing was impossible.

But, an insidious voice from deep within whispered, *people do change. I've changed. Maybe he has too.*

Not so much that he'd lost the ability to take advantage of any weakness in an opponent and move in for the kill.

They had parted bitterly and she'd assumed that Devin had cut his losses.

Yet tonight he'd said he wanted her back.

She dried her face and frowned at her reflection in the mirror. Could she believe that he'd simply missed her, and that seeing her again had triggered renewed feelings, perhaps as powerful and disturbing as those he'd aroused in her?

He hadn't mentioned love, she recalled uneasily, hanging up the towel. He'd always found her sexually stimulating and still did, no doubt about that. Her skin tingled at the remembrance of the lambent flame in his eyes.

Had she really expected that he would give her money for nothing?

No, he'd have his pound of flesh. Her flesh.

Shannon shook herself. It would be a crazy situation to put herself in. Crazy. Only a masochist would do it.

And she was no masochist.

In the hour before sleep rescued her, and throughout next day, she couldn't stop herself from going over and over the conversation. Couldn't school her body to indifference at the memory of the unexpected kiss.

All the following week, in any moment she could spare from working on a TV commercial she been commissioned to direct, she revisited every avenue that she'd already exhausted of raising the money she needed, but even the modest success of *Heart of the Wilderness* wasn't enough to open any doors, except for vague suggestions to resubmit her proposal the following year.

The commercial involved children, dogs and endless bars of chocolate. It paid the rent, but after five days Shannon was exhausted, never wanted to see another chocolate bar, and was less than enamoured of both children and dogs.

Anyway, children had long been on the list of things she preferred not to think about too much.

On Friday night she was lying propped against cushions on her couch, drinking coffee and poring over the script of her beloved project. As she scribbled notes on the pages, thinking about camera shots and angles, she had to wonder why she bothered. Odds were that the Hobbs story was going to be filmed by someone else, and her dream would die.

When the telephone rang she picked up the receiver listlessly and gave her name.

'Shannon,' said a deep, well-remembered voice.

Instantly all her senses were alert. She sat up. 'Devin?'

'How are you?'

'I'm…fine.'

'Are you alone?'

'Yes.' Why did he want to know?

'I haven't heard from you.'

'No.' There wasn't much she could add to that. Once or twice she'd toyed with the idea of leaving a blunt, even rude, repudiation of his offer on the answer machine, and at other times she'd been tempted to tell him she'd accept any terms he cared to lay down. But her silence should have told him she had no intention of taking up his preposterous offer.

After a short pause he said, 'Have you found a backer?'

'No.'

'Feel like going out for supper?'

'I'm tired.' True. 'I've had a hectic week.'

'Me too. I could bring a pizza and come round.' His voice dropped into seduction mode. 'Pepperoni, pineapple, black olives…'

He knew all her weaknesses. She hadn't thought she was hungry, but now her mouth was watering.

While she was still trying to muster the will to say no, he said, 'I'll be there in about half an hour. And I promise not to keep you up late.'

He'd hung up before she could say anything more. She put down the phone and sat staring at the page on her lap without seeing it.

Maybe he'd had second thoughts about financing her film, decided to retract his outrageous terms.

Some hope, she told herself. More likely he still hoped to talk her into accepting them.

'When they're ice-skating in hell,' she muttered.

It was only twenty-five minutes before the doorbell buzzed. The aroma of melted cheese met her nostrils as soon as she opened the door, bringing back memories of evenings when they'd sat side by side watching a film on TV while sharing a pizza and a bottle of wine.

He'd brought wine too, her favourite red. It was raining outside, a light, misty drizzle that dewed the wine bottle. Tiny sparklets of moisture glittered in Devon's dark hair under the glow of the hall light.

He wore no jacket or tie with his blue shirt and dark trousers. Her eyes were level with the open neck of the shirt, and she could see the tiny pulse beating under lightly tanned skin. Her own pulses quickened.

She led him into the lounge before it occurred to her that it would have been safer to eat in the dining area in the kitchen. This room was far too cosy.

But he'd already placed the pizza and wine on the coffee table, beside the script. 'A corkscrew?' he enquired.

Shannon turned to the old oak sideboard and extracted a corkscrew, two wineglasses and a couple of plates. Pretty, flowered china plates that had once belonged to her grandmother, and that her mother had bequeathed to her.

Devin sat on the ruby-red armchair and deftly opened the bottle. As she resumed her seat on the sofa he poured the wine and placed a glass in front of Shannon, then lifted the lid of the box and slid a slice of pizza onto a plate.

Automatically Shannon tucked her bare feet under her on the couch before biting into the layers of cheese, extras and the doughy crust. 'Mmm,' she murmured as the concoction released its flavour onto her tongue.

Devin smiled, watching her. Then he took a bite of his own piece, picked up his glass and leaned back in the chair.

Shannon swallowed. 'How did you know this is what I needed?'

'I know a lot about you, Shannon.'

She supposed he did, superficially. But he had never shared her deepest feelings. He didn't understand why she'd been compelled to end their marriage. Her clumsy efforts to explain had only made him angry.

He seemed mellower now, the anger dissipated by time.

Devin dusted crumbs from his hands. 'A script?' he asked, nodding at the open folder on the table. 'The one you're wanting finance for?'

'Yes.'

'May I?'

She nodded and he picked it up, taking another slice of pizza as he began reading.

Shannon let him do so in silence, watching as he put down his plate with the half-eaten slice on it and turned a page, apparently forgetting to finish the food.

Hardly glancing up, he drank some wine, then poured himself more and went on reading.

Shannon took another slice and nibbled at it while covertly studying his face.

Frustratingly, his expression scarcely changed, except for an occasional frown of concentration, or a faint lift of the decisive black brows. She finished eating and sat very still, not wanting to disturb him. The remaining pizza cooled and congealed and still he read on.

Near the end he stood up, the script still in his

hands, and walked across the room, then on reaching the window he turned and bent his head over the pages again.

When at last he closed the folder and looked at her, he said, 'This really happened?'

'The court scenes are almost verbatim transcripts. The script's based on them and the newspaper reports at the time.'

'They found the man guilty on that evidence?'

'Uh-huh.'

He came back to his chair and dropped into it, looking down at the folder in his hands before returning it to the table. 'And no one is interested?'

'Not with me as the director anyway,' she admitted wryly. 'But I can't stop other people using the public record. Then I'll have missed my chance.'

Devin leaned forward and picked up his half-empty wineglass. Considering the red depths, he said, 'You needn't if you accept my offer.'

So he hadn't changed his mind. 'On your terms?'

He looked up then, his mouth curving in a smile that held little real humour. 'You said it was a business proposition. Well, that's the way business works, my sweet. The golden rule—the one with the gold makes the rules.'

'I thought the golden rule was, "Do unto others…"'

'As they would do unto you if they had half a chance.'

Shannon shook her head. 'That's a bleak philosophy. And I don't believe you subscribe to it.'

He looked at her with a scoffing lift to his brows. 'Don't kid yourself. I'm no soft touch, not even for you.'

He'd already shown that by his outrageous demands in return for the money she needed.

'I didn't think you were,' she said.

It entered her mind that she could try meeting him on his own ground. 'But maybe we could negotiate.'

A spark of surprise lit his eyes before he hid it under lowered lids, regarding her consideringly. 'The main condition is non-negotiable.'

'That I live with you?'

'As my wife.'

'Meaning,' Shannon lifted her head, 'that you expect me to sleep with you. Have sex.'

'Among other things.'

'Whenever you want?'

He frowned. 'When we mutually want it.'

'Suppose I don't want it at all?'

He looked at her with a hint of derision. 'Forgive me, Shannon. I find it difficult to suppose anything of the sort.'

The hairs on the back of her neck rose. 'Maybe you're over-confident. Will you promise that if I say no you'll respect my wishes?'

His shoulders seemed to stiffen subtly. 'When,' he asked softly, dangerously, 'have I ever forced you?'

Never. He had never needed to. She'd been eager

and willing to make love with him, let him weave his insidious magic, weave her own about him in return, and on the few occasions she didn't feel up to it he'd been patient, putting aside his physical frustration out of concern for her. Even after they'd begun to grow apart, and their marriage had started to crumble, sex had been the one tenuous thread holding them together.

'I just need to know,' she said, 'what exactly you want for your money. What it is you're buying.'

His mouth went grim. 'I want a wife. In every sense of the word. Not a slave, Shannon.'

'For the duration of the filming.'

There was a pause before he nodded. 'That's the deal.'

'And then I'll be free to go? My debt discharged?'

'Certainly.' His voice grated.

Shannon looked at the folder on the table. She wanted to do that story so badly her mouth watered, the taste of it almost as tangible as the cheese flavour that still lingered on her tongue.

She swallowed. 'You have to understand that I'll be filming, sometimes at odd hours. Maybe on location.'

He nodded again, curtly. 'I won't stand in your way. As your husband, I hope I'll be welcome to go along and watch sometimes.'

Her eyes widened. 'Go along? With me?'

'I'd like to keep an eye on my investment.'

That sounded believable. Which investment, though? she wondered cynically—the film or herself?

As graciously as she could, she said, 'You'd be welcome to visit the set, so long as you don't interfere with the filming.'

'I wouldn't dream of interfering in a field where I have no expertise. I'd merely be an interested observer.'

She could hardly deny him the right. Not if he had millions of dollars sunk into the project. 'And you wouldn't want any control over casting or hiring?' she persisted.

He hesitated, his eyes sharpening. 'I'm sure you'll be guided by what's best for the film.'

No doubt about that. He must know that was the first consideration for her.

'Any more questions?' Devin asked.

She couldn't think of any. Impossible to believe though it was, she was seriously beginning to think she had no choice but to take his outrageous offer.

Her mouth felt dry, and her heart was pounding, unnaturally loudly. She parted her lips and moistened them with her tongue. 'All right,' she heard herself say. 'It's a deal.'

For a long moment Devin sat motionless, as if he hadn't heard. She began to think that the words had only been in her head.

Then she saw his throat move as he swallowed, before he leaned across and poured more wine into her empty glass, his hand perfectly steady. He lifted his own glass and said, 'Shall we drink to that?'

Shannon picked up her glass as if in a dream, half expecting to wake any minute and find that it was. The wine, blood-red and reflecting the light from the overhead lamp, danced against the sides of the glass, and she realised her hand was shaking. Hastily she raised the drink to her lips, nearly choking on the gasping gulp she took.

Devin replaced his glass on the table. 'I'll see my lawyer about drawing up a contract. You're welcome to discuss it with your own legal representative. But our…private arrangement won't be in writing.' He paused. 'As soon as the formal agreement is signed and you move in I'll arrange an initial transfer of funds to your account. The remainder will be paid as it's needed.'

'Th-thank you,' Shannon said, her head whirling, and not from the wine. *It isn't too late to back out,* a panicky little voice inside her said. *Tell him you didn't mean it.* She opened her mouth to say she'd changed her mind. But nothing came out.

'Of course,' Devin was saying, 'if you prefer to come to me sooner, you're welcome anytime.'

Dumbly she shook her head. 'No. Not before…'

Not before she had to. Not until the contract on which this bizarre bargain rested had been signed and sealed.

'That's it, then.' He put down his glass and stood up again. 'I'll let you know when it's ready for signing.'

Shannon stood up too. Going ahead of him to open the door, she held her head high.

As she waited for him to pass her, he slipped a hand under her chin, lifting her face to him.

Shannon stiffened, her eyes meeting his defiantly. 'We don't have a contract yet.'

His mouth moved, more a grimace than a smile. 'So hands off until we do?' He studied her, his gaze playing over her face as if memorising it. 'You drive a hard bargain.'

'I thought you of all people would respect that.'

Devin laughed then, briefly, before he dropped his hand and turned, striding out the door and down the path without looking back. Shannon closed it, let out a breath and went back to the living room. The empty glasses and the remains of the pizza on the table, the lingering aroma of cheese, convinced her that this was reality, not some weird fantasy.

She took up the script and hugged it to her like a shield. If she could make this come to life on screen, that was worth almost anything.

Almost.

Devin phoned on Tuesday. 'Can you get to a meeting in my lawyer's office this afternoon at three-thirty?'

'That's quick,' she said.

'I told him we're in a hurry. You are, aren't you?'

'Yes.' She supposed that when you were a millionaire in a hurry even lawyers jumped to your bidding.

'I can pick you up,' he offered.

'No, I'll drive myself. Are they still in Parnell?'

'No, I changed to another firm last year.'

The practice was a large one and she had no trouble finding the office in the centre of town. When she gave her name at the desk, even though she was a few minutes early the receptionist said, 'Oh, yes. Mr Keynes is already with Mr Symonds. They're expecting you.'

The contract seemed simple enough, and she suspected that the lawyer thought Devin was being unwise investing in such a risky venture. To an outsider she seemed to be getting a lot of money with no security, the only safeguard being the stipulation that accounts were to be strictly kept and regularly presented for audit.

The man questioned her discreetly as to her experience and financial circumstances, and she gave him frank answers. She saw his covert glance at Devin, then at her, and the flash of enlightenment that dawned. 'I wish you luck,' he said finally. 'It's wise to have these things on a formal footing, even if the arrangement is between…ah…friends.'

Devin gave him a keen look in return. He said coolly, 'Shannon is my wife.'

The man's face, for just an instant, was a study in shock. 'Your wife?' he repeated, and then hastily, 'Ah, I see. Congratulations.'

Of course he didn't see. He had no idea of the hidden part of this agreement.

Shannon threw a furious glare at Devin but he seemed impervious. Turning to her, he said, 'Do you want to run it by your own lawyer?'

She wanted to get out of there. Anyway, there was no point in quibbling. As he'd said, he had the money and she wanted it. And he and his legal eagle hadn't slipped in anything she could see that she might reasonably object to. 'No,' she said. 'I'll sign it now.'

She and Devin left the office together. In the carpeted elevator on the way down she said, 'Did you need to tell him that we were married?'

'He thought you were my mistress,' he said. 'Would you have preferred him to go on thinking it?'

It would have been closer to the truth, she reflected, shame twisting in her stomach. The fact that they happened to have a marriage certificate merely lent a spurious respectability to what she'd called a sordid arrangement. In truth, she was no different from any other woman who slept with a man for money.

Except that Devin had specifically promised he wouldn't coerce her into sex. So if she didn't want to share his bed he had only himself to blame, she thought, squaring her shoulders. She would live with him, but he'd agreed that sex had to be mutual. And how could she sleep with a man who had paid for the privilege?

A Catch-22 situation.

He might find himself hoist on his own petard. Maybe she could survive this with her self-respect intact.

CHAPTER FOUR

IN THE marble-floored foyer, Devin said, 'Do you need help to pack?'

'I don't want any help. Anyway, it'll take me a week or so to get organised. I know an actress who's looking for a place and she might take over my flat while I'm away, but I'll have to consult my landlord. I can't do everything in a day or two.'

'If you have furniture you want to bring—'

'I couldn't park my furniture in your apartment.' Her old bow-fronted sideboard, her cheerful chairs, would clash with the carefully co-ordinated decor of his home and spoil its elegant minimalism. 'I'll bring my clothes,' she said. 'That's all I need. The rest of my stuff can stay where it is.'

'As you like. But the sooner you move in the sooner you get the money.'

'Don't push me, Devin!' she flashed. 'This is hard enough for me as it is.'

Quietly he said, 'I don't mean to put the screws on.'

'You already have.' But he was making it possible for her to fulfil her dream. Grudgingly she added, 'Not that I'm not…grateful for your help.'

Devin laughed. 'That hurt, didn't it? I don't want your gratitude, Shannon. All I want is you.'

The words echoed in her mind, and she remembered he'd used them before in different circumstances. Just days before their wedding she'd wondered if he didn't regret asking her to marry him; she'd said he could have had any number of women who were more beautiful, more glamorous, more accustomed to moving in the inner circle of Auckland's moneyed classes—in every way more suitable for a man with his background, living his kind of life.

He'd brushed aside her worries and kissed her with passion and purpose, murmuring into her hair afterwards, while she was still surfacing from almost drowning in pleasure, 'All I want is you.'

She'd believed him then. She supposed he'd believed it himself. A deep sadness at what they'd lost swept over her. 'I'll let you know when I'm ready to move in,' she said.

As she made to turn away, he caught at her arm. 'Don't leave it too long.'

The actress was delighted to move into Shannon's flat, and the landlord had no objections. She had to give her new address and phone number to a few people, and some eyebrows were raised. Most of them would deduce it was unlikely she could afford a luxury apartment.

It wouldn't be possible to keep her living arrangements a secret for long, but her moving in with Devin would be a nine days' wonder, and then some other juicy gossip would take its place.

Craig had been unexpectedly put out. She let him into the flat only an hour after phoning to tell him the film would go ahead after all, and he found her packing her clothes.

'You're going back to him?' he asked incredulously. 'Why?'

'It was your idea for me to go and see him,' she said. 'When we met again we…we talked, and decided to give our marriage another go.'

'Is he handing over the money for the film?'

'Yes. He's being…um…generous.'

'Bribing you.'

'It's not like that!' But she was guiltily conscious that it was almost exactly like that. 'We realised that…that we've both grown, changed.'

'Did you sleep with him?'

'Craig!'

'Sorry, sorry.' He raised his hands, backing away. 'Not my business.'

'We came to an understanding. He read the script, and decided he'd like to invest in it. Our personal…um…affairs are a separate matter, and I don't want to discuss them.'

'Yeah, well…' Craig still looked vaguely suspicious. 'What's this guy like, anyway? What did he do to make you leave him before?'

'He didn't do anything. I mean, we just didn't agree on some things.'

'What sort of things?'

Shannon shrugged. 'Marriage. Life. My career.' *Babies…* 'You know, trivial things like that.'

'Oh, yeah.' Craig looked at her fixedly. 'So do you agree now?'

Very unlikely. 'I don't know. That's what we want to find out.'

Was that what Devin wanted? Or was he just exercising his power because she'd refused to bow to pressure before and now he had her in a position where he could make the rules and she had no choice but to obey them?

She shivered, instinctively wrapping her arms about herself.

'You're not cold, are you?' Craig asked in surprise.

'No. Do you still want to play the witness in this film?'

That was enough to take his mind off anything else. His face brightening, he said, 'Hell, yeah! You know I do.'

She moved into Devin's apartment on Saturday morning. He came to the lobby and carried two suitcases up for her while she followed with her laptop computer, a shoulder pack and an overnight bag.

Devin led the way into a large room with a low king-size bed against one wall, its cover patterned in maroon, black and silver. He put down the luggage at the foot of the bed as Shannon stopped inside the door, then he came back to her, easing the pack from her shoulder and taking the computer and overnight bag. 'Is this all?'

'Yes.' She looked around, saw a long dressing table with a man's hairbrush on top, a dark jacket lying on a maroon-leather stool. 'But this is your room.'

'Ours.' He placed the computer on the bed and the other bags with the suitcases. 'Welcome home, Shannon.'

Shannon stayed stubbornly where she stood. 'It isn't my home,' she said. 'And this isn't *our* room. Surely in an apartment this size you have more than one bedroom.'

His eyes cooled. 'Three, and a study. I thought you might like to use one of the bedrooms for your workroom, office, whatever. The other is a guest room.'

'Then I'll have that,' she said, and turned to go and look for it.

He was beside her in two strides, his hand on her arm swinging her round, his eyes the colour of storm clouds. 'You're my wife, Shannon. No separate bedrooms.'

'You promised I didn't have to have sex with you.' She tried to pull away but his grip was unrelenting.

He looked over at the huge bed. 'You won't even have to touch me if you don't want to,' he said witheringly. 'But we are going to sleep together. As in spend the nights side by side.'

No way. It was going to be difficult enough living together. Sleeping in the same bed would be sheer torture. She said, 'Plenty of married couples have separate bedrooms.'

'We never did. And we're not going to start now.'

Her head lifted. 'I didn't agree to this!'

'You agreed to abide by my terms. They were clear enough.'

'And I thought *I'd* made it clear that I don't want to share a bed.'

'You never said that.'

'You knew what I meant!'

'Lesson number two of business practice,' he said. 'Don't take anything for granted.'

'Isn't that what *you* are doing?'

He smiled. 'I'm the one holding the cards. I haven't written that cheque yet.'

'That's cheating! You can't make new conditions now!'

'Aren't you the one who's cheating?' he challenged her. 'Trying to have your cake and eat it? I spelled it out for you, Shannon. We live as husband and wife. That doesn't include forced sex, but it does mean sleeping together…literally.'

'I can't!' She tried again to free herself, and he relaxed his hold.

Stepping back, she fought unreasonable trepidation.

'You can't fulfil the terms of our contract?' He folded his arms, looking at her with a steely gaze.

She knew what that meant. No money, and no film. Could she hold him to the terms of the formal, of-

ficial version that they'd both signed? After all, no one
else knew about their private agreement.

Taking him to court would cost her money that she
didn't have. And time. Besides, Devin could be ruth-
less when he chose, just witness what he was doing
now. Although essentially a private person, he hated
to lose, and he'd probably grit his teeth and allow their
verbal contract to be aired in public if necessary.
Shannon didn't fancy being known as the woman
who'd sold her soul for money.

As he'd said, the bed was easily big enough for two
people to share without even touching.

Shutting out an interior voice that was asking who
else he'd shared that enormous bed with, she gritted
her teeth. 'If you insist. But I'm keeping you to your
promise.'

That first night she went to bed early, pleading tired-
ness. Devin glanced up from the financial magazine
he'd brought into the living room to read, and nodded
at her. 'Goodnight.'

After putting on gold satin pyjamas Shannon lay
awake in the darkness for some time, tensing when
she heard movement in the other room, but then there
was silence and eventually she slipped into sleep.

When she woke in the morning there was a dent in
the pillow beside her and the covers were neatly folded
back on that side of the bed. The shower next door
was running, but in a few moments it stopped and
Devin stepped into the bedroom, his hair damp and

tousled. He'd tucked a towel about his waist—an unexpected formality in deference, she supposed, to her presence.

He said, 'Sleep all right?'

'Yes.' She looked at the clock by the bed and sat up, throwing off the covers. 'Have you finished with the bathroom?'

'All yours.' Devin was looking at her critically. 'Pyjamas?'

She'd never worn them when they were together, preferring impractical, sexy wisps of satin, lawn and lace. Devin hadn't been a pyjama man either, and if he wore anything at all in bed it was usually satin shorts.

'I like these,' she said defiantly. She had taken a fancy to the rich colour and fabric and bought them on impulse, but hadn't worn them much. Last night they'd seemed the most suitable attire for sleeping beside a man she had no intention of having sex with. Maybe she'd buy some more.

'Do you have a chastity belt underneath?' he inquired caustically.

Already on her way to the bathroom, Shannon cast him a scornful look. 'I don't need one to resist your charms,' she shot at him, before scurrying through the door and quickly locking herself in. On the other side she heard him laugh.

When she emerged he was gone, but the smell of frying bacon emanated from the kitchen. He'd made breakfast for two, just as he used to every Sunday they were together.

He served it in the kitchen. Watching her appraisal of the stark tiles, dark granite and gleaming stainless steel, he said, 'You can pretty it up if you like. Hang your bunches of garlic and dried chillies, and put potted herbs around.'

'You wouldn't mind?' Not that she'd have time anyway while she was filming. And she'd be out of here in a few months.

'Do whatever you like,' Devin said. 'This is your home, I told you.'

Temporarily. Despising herself for a ripple of melancholy at the reminder, she pushed it back into her subconscious where it belonged.

The first payment appeared the following day in the bank account she'd created for the film expenses and Shannon started working toward a shooting date. She spent hours on the telephone and in meetings. If nothing else, it left little waking time to be with Devin, for which she should have been grateful.

At the end of the week Devin said, 'I have a business party next Wednesday night. One of my subsidiaries is opening new premises and I'd like you to come if you can make the time.'

'Certainly,' she said coolly. 'What do you want me to wear?'

'It wasn't an order,' he said, his voice deceptively mild. 'Only an invitation.'

'I'm sorry, it's hard to know the difference…in this situation.'

'Wear something pretty,' he said shortly. 'It's not a black-tie affair. If you need to buy a new dress use my credit card. I've arranged a facility for you.'

She stared at him. 'I don't need it. I'll try to dress up to your standard.'

'You know I wasn't criticising.'

'It sounded as though you were afraid I might disgrace you.'

'Oh, for God's sake, Shannon! I just thought you might want to treat yourself. I wish you'd stop reading some ulterior motive into everything.'

'I'll try not to,' she said, ultra-polite, 'but sometimes it's difficult, you understand.'

'Give it a rest, will you?'

'Whatever you say.' Her tone was dulcet, and he lifted his gaze to the ceiling before returning it to her, his eyes shimmering with reluctant, angry humour.

Shannon walked toward the door and he moved aside to let her pass.

She paused, tilting her head to look up at him. 'Goodnight, Devin.'

'Goodnight.' He had his hands jammed firmly into his pockets and there was a faint lift to his lips, an amused challenge in his eyes. He looked handsome and arrogant and far too sure of himself. Her spine straightened and she swept past him, ignoring the little hot shiver down her back that told her he was still watching.

*   *   *

The dress she wore to his business function was moss-green satin with a silvery glow. Deceptively simple and almost seamless, it clung to her body and swirled about her legs, and when she joined him in the living room Devin said, 'I always liked that. I'm glad you kept it.'

She liked it too. It made her feel feminine and pretty without being overdressed, and was a change from her workaday jeans and colourful tops.

The evening was a bit of a strain at first. Several people couldn't conceal their initial surprise when Devin introduced her as his wife, but they were friendly enough, and a few who remembered her even seemed pleased to see her again.

Some recalled her name being mentioned in reviews, and a number had seen *Heart of the Wilderness*. Their genuine interest made it easier to carry on a conversation.

'You were quite a hit tonight,' Devin told her as he drove them home afterwards.

'A hit?' She turned to look at him.

'I was congratulated several times on my beautiful, talented wife. I hope you weren't too bored?'

'As a matter of fact, it was an interesting evening.'

'That's new.'

'What is?'

'You never found anything interesting or enjoyable in these business-related affairs before.'

'I was too nervous to enjoy them back then.'

'Nervous?' he queried. 'Why?'

'All those go-getting high-flyers are a bit over-whelming in groups. I was a fish out of water.' Ignorant of the higher echelons of commerce, unsure of herself among university-educated people knowledgeably discussing current affairs or the fine arts, she had confined herself to nods and vague, glassy smiles that concealed a deep-seated dread of making a fool of herself. 'And I was younger then,' she reminded him. 'Only twenty-two.'

Three years more experienced and with an increasingly successful career, she had developed a new confidence and tonight, since the other guests had no qualms about revealing their lack of knowledge of her craft, she'd freely questioned them in turn without fear of being written off as a complete idiot.

Devin looked at her again, searchingly. 'I never knew you felt that way.'

'I did my best to hide it.'

'You could have told me.'

'I was embarrassed. I wanted you to be proud of me.'

Even private occasions had been an ordeal. Devin's long-time friends came from a world of privilege that was alien to her, and few had taken the trouble to make her feel at ease. Perhaps, like him, they hadn't been aware of her insecurity.

He reached out and took her hand, his fingers curling about hers. 'I was always proud of you. I'm afraid

I lack imagination—I've never been very good at guessing people's feelings.'

She supposed that was true. Devin was at home with machinery and things he could touch, and with figures that behaved logically, predictably. He'd shown his feelings for her in physical ways, with his hands and his body. But emotions were foreign territory and he rarely revealed them himself, except in the privacy of their bedroom.

Lovemaking had been the only thing that broke through his unnerving control. Following his lead and wanting to please him, she'd entered into it with eagerness and joy, liberated from the inhibition that she'd learned early to impose on other feelings like sadness and need, finding that intense pleasure could at least temporarily banish them.

But she had been afraid of displaying negative emotion. Perhaps if she'd expressed herself more freely, their relationship might have fared better.

She fought a desire to lean her head on his shoulder. Her fingers moved in his and he released them, perhaps thinking she was trying to escape.

When they arrived in the underground garage and he opened the car door for her, one of her unaccustomed high heels caught in the edge of the mat as she stepped out, and Devin swooped to hold her, his arm about her waist.

Instinctively she clutched at his sleeve to steady herself. Her face almost touched the lapels of his jacket, and she breathed in a faint scent of aftershave and musk. He didn't immediately let go, and she lifted her eyes to meet his dark, fiery gaze, quickly veiled by lowering lids as he looked at her mouth.

Then another car roared into the garage, its garish lights sweeping over them, and even as she stiffened Devin swore under his breath and let her go.

In the elevator they stood apart, not looking at each other, and when they reached the apartment Shannon bade him a subdued goodnight and went straight to the bedroom. She was asleep by the time Devin joined her there.

Devin showed an interest in Shannon's plans that he'd never displayed before. She supposed it made a difference that he had so much money sunk into the end product.

Some evenings they would sit talking, he with his long legs stretched out before him while he leaned back in a wide leather chair, a shot glass in hand, she with her feet tucked up beside her on a couch as she told him about her pre-production progress.

After listening to her describe the exhaustive process of checking locations that the production manager had found, and discussing with the art director if they looked or could be made to look authentically nineteenth century, he said, 'What about the actors?'

Outsiders always thought the actors were the most important ingredient. It was often their names that drew people to see a film, yet weeks before the cameras began to roll the production team had been working to have everything in place.

'There's one major problem. I had someone in mind to play the witness's fiancée, but she got a better offer while I was trying to get finance.' Shannon and the casting director had auditioned a number of hopefuls since but none stood out as completely right.

'And the male lead, the witness?'

'Craig of course, bless him.' Her voice grew soft. 'He won't let me down.'

Devin swirled the drink in his glass. 'Wouldn't it be better to get someone with an international reputation if you hope to sell the film overseas?'

'This could be the film that will *make* Craig into an international star. It's happened to others.'

'So he's not simply doing it for love?'

'No one can live on love. He does love the script though, and it's nice that this time I can pay him decently. The others too.' She added wistfully, 'It certainly would help, having a big name on the cast list. But those guys make megabucks.' She sighed, and added thoughtfully, 'Though sometimes they work for peanuts if they like a script enough.' Tilting her head a little, she queried half-humorously, 'I don't suppose you happen to know any young female Hollywood stars?'

'As a matter of fact,' he said quite casually, 'I do know one. Rose Grady is…an old friend.'

Shannon blinked at him. The New Zealand actress had made her first Hollywood film a couple of years ago and been nominated for an Oscar. 'You never said…!'

'I was at university with her brother. Rose and I had a thing going for a while back then.'

Jealousy brushed Shannon with its poisoned wings.

She pushed it aside. 'You never mentioned you knew her when…'

He threw her an ironic look, waiting for her to finish the sentence, but when she didn't he said, 'She wasn't famous when you and I were together, and anyway, I hadn't seen her for years until I looked her up in L.A. when I had a delayed flight. Since then I've often spent time with her. She's always saying she'd like to come home for a while.'

'Why hasn't she?'

'Pressure of work.' He shrugged. 'You'd understand that.'

Ignoring the pointed remark, Shannon said, 'I don't suppose she'd be interested, even if she could spare the time.' Which as he'd just intimated was highly unlikely. Although, she admitted to herself, Rose Grady was exactly the type that the part demanded. 'Anyway, we can't afford her. The budget wouldn't go anywhere near her price.'

He looked thoughtful. 'I could ask her. Maybe she'll like the script enough to work for peanuts. I'll be going to America in the next couple of weeks.'

That was news to her, but she supposed he travelled so frequently it was routine to him. 'For how long?'

'Five days or so. Will you miss me?'

'I'll be busy anyway.' Looking away from him, she wondered how much of the four or five days he'd be spending with his 'old friend,' and tried to tell herself it didn't matter. Returning her gaze to him, she asked, 'You'll be…seeing her?' And despite her effort to keep her tone neutral, it came out on a disconcertingly accusing note.

He gave her a penetrating look. 'I'm not going to be "seeing" other women while we're together, Shannon, if that's what you mean. Except in a strictly platonic sense.'

'I didn't mean to imply anything,' she denied. 'You're free to do as you like.'

'I don't believe in open marriages.' He paused. 'So I hope you don't think that you are "free" in that sense.'

'I have other things to think about than sex.'

'Obviously.' His mouth went tight. 'Are you telling me you wouldn't be concerned if I were sleeping with other women?'

How could she say the very thought made her feel sick—and furious? After all, she was denying him what used to be called a man's marital rights. 'As long as you're discreet,' she said with difficulty, 'I won't complain.'

'Oh, you won't?' he said grimly. 'Then you wouldn't mind if I brought another woman here for the night?'

The hair at the back of her neck tingled. 'I didn't say you could flaunt your affairs in my face!'

'There won't be any affairs!' He stood up, and in two strides was leaning over her, his hands on the back of the sofa, trapping her. His eyes blazed. 'Not on my part and not on yours. Is that clear?'

CHAPTER FIVE

'OR WHAT?' Shannon defied him, her own eyes angry. 'What are you going to do? Beat me?'

'Don't tempt me.' Devin straightened. 'You know damn well I wouldn't physically abuse you. But I won't stand by and let you break our agreement in spirit or in principle. You're sailing dangerously close to the wind as it is.'

'Is that a threat?'

Of course it was. If he withheld the rest of the money he'd promised, the whole project would fall apart. She supposed she was lucky he hadn't used the possibility to coerce her into sex.

He shoved both hands into his pockets. 'I'm not threatening you, Shannon. It's a reminder that you're still my wife and you promised to act as such…at least for a time.'

'How could I forget?' she flung at him, still angry. 'I'm living with you, aren't I? Sleeping in the same bed.'

'Do you hate it so much?' He looked down at her, his eyes veiled by the dark, straight lashes.

There were times when she didn't, when they nearly slipped back into the companionship they'd enjoyed years ago. But always there was the knowledge that the so-called reconciliation was artificial. 'Of course I hate it,' she answered him. 'What do you expect when you know you got me here against my will?' Her deep chagrin and resentment that he had manipulated her into accepting his condition added to the undercurrent of tension between them.

He continued looking at her for several seconds, and then turned and walked across the room to the big window with its magnificent view of the harbour. 'What would you have done,' he said remotely, 'if I'd simply asked you to come back, try to rebuild our marriage?'

She didn't know. If she'd any sense she would have refused to put herself through that, with the distinct probability of reliving months of disillusion and pain. But he had given her no choice. Or rather, had made the choice into a humiliating quid pro quo. And that was hard to forgive, impossible to forget. A lump in her throat impeding her voice, she said acridly, 'You'll never know, will you? It's too late now to find out.'

And with that she got up and left him standing at the window with the dark night sky behind him.

The following evening Devin hadn't yet come home when the telephone rang just before nine and Shannon answered it.

There was a short silence, then an older woman's voice said, 'Shannon?'

Her spine stiffened. 'Yes,' she said. 'How are you, Marcia?'

'I'm well…thank you,' Devin's mother said. '*What* are you doing there?'

Living with your son. 'Devin hasn't told you?' Shannon said, silently cursing him. 'We're…together again. For a while.'

'A *while?*' Marcia Keynes' voice rose slightly above its usually modulated tone. 'What does that mean?'

'We…we're having a trial reconciliation.' Devin's euphemism was as good as any. 'Can I give him a message?'

'He's…you're…thinking of getting married again?'

'We were never actually divorced,' Shannon pointed out. Another echo of Devin.

'As good as,' his mother said tartly. 'After all, you left him, didn't you?' she accused. 'Do you mean you've changed your mind?'

'It was Devin's idea,' Shannon said.

'Well…I must say you've surprised me.'

And she clearly wasn't pleased.

'Shall I give him a message?' Shannon offered again, not anxious to prolong this conversation.

After a short silence Marcia said stiltedly, 'I wanted to be sure he hadn't forgotten his father's birthday dinner on Friday. Perhaps you would ask him to ring me when he comes in?'

'Certainly.' Shannon wondered if he would, and face up to a cross-examination from his mother.

'Thank you. Goodnight.'

The phone clicked in her ear, and Shannon replaced the receiver with a faint, wry twist to her mouth.

When Devin came in an hour later she said, 'Your mother phoned to remind you of your father's birthday party. She didn't know I was living here.'

'I haven't seen my parents since you moved in.'

'You didn't think to pick up the phone and tell them?'

'No. What did she say to you?'

'She didn't say anything much. She'd like you to call her back.'

'Tonight?' Devin glanced at his watch.

'I think she'll be waiting up until you do.'

He picked up the portable receiver from the telephone and dialled, crossing to the cabinet that held drinks. Glancing at Shannon he asked, 'Would you like something?'

'A red wine, thanks.' Obviously he wasn't bothering to make the phone call private.

He poured the wine one-handed and gave it to her as he said into the phone, 'Mother…Shannon said you wanted to speak to me.'

Turning away, he returned to pour a wine for himself. 'Yes, we are…no, it's quite recent…I've been busy.'

He sat down opposite Shannon and shifted the receiver a little to sip his drink. 'I hadn't forgotten. I'll be there—with Shannon if she's free.'

Even as Shannon looked up, startled, his voice hardened. 'She's my wife, Mother. If I'm invited, so is

Shannon.' Then after a second or two, 'Thank you. Why don't you ask her yourself?'

Shannon made an agitated signal of negation but he ignored it, passing her the phone.

Reluctantly she took it from him. 'Marcia?'

'Shannon…of course you're welcome to join us on Friday,' Marcia said coolly. 'Ralph will be pleased to see you again.'

Marcia had obviously had a battle between her instinct and her rigidly entrenched good manners, but couldn't quite bring herself to pretend that she ever wanted to see her son's ex-wife again. Devin's father, though, had what his wife called with a sort of acerbic tolerance 'an eye for a pretty face,' and after a rocky beginning Shannon had got along quite well with him.

'Thank you.' Shannon tried to sound grateful, while glaring at Devin. 'That's very…kind,' she added before handing back the phone to him.

He rang off almost immediately, and she said, 'There was no need for that. Of course I won't go.'

'Why not?'

'Because I don't like being where I'm not wanted, for one thing.'

'What makes you think you're not wanted?'

She cast him a glance full of scorn. 'You forced her into inviting me.'

'No one has to force my mother to remember the normal courtesies. She just takes a while to adjust to a new situation.'

Marcia had never adjusted to his marriage, but

Shannon held her tongue about that. 'I won't go,' she said again. 'It's a family occasion.'

'You are family,' Devin insisted. 'And I'd like you to be there.'

'Whatever for? Just to prove you only have to whistle and I'll come to heel?'

His voice was mild but his eyes had cooled. 'I want my family to see that we're together.'

'Rubbing their noses in it? They already know you can't be made to conform to what they want. I think that's half the reason you married me in the first place. You knew they'd disapprove and you wanted to fling me in their faces.'

Impatience lit his eyes. 'When I met you I was way past the teenage rebellion stage. You know perfectly well I fell for you hook, line and sinker. The last thing on my mind was using you as some kind of weapon.'

'You told me what a struggle it was to strike out on your own, your father assuming you'd go into the family firm and eventually take over from him.'

'My sister will make a much better fist of it. Her heart's in the printing business, and mine never was.'

'They use your machines.'

'Because they're the best on the market. I never asked for any favours and was never given any.'

'So why are you determined that your family has to accept me? They never thought I was good enough for you and they're hardly likely to change their minds now. What's the point?'

'No one ever said you weren't good enough!'

'No one needed to. They're far too polite to spell out what was blindingly obvious.'

His mother's delicate interrogation and pityingly raised eyebrows had certainly implied that a farmer's daughter from the wilds of Northland with no living relatives and no proper 'background' was hardly a suitable bride for a Keynes.

Shannon had been twelve when her mother died after a short, painful illness, and she'd done her best to help her father keep the farm going. At sixteen she'd left school, and although jobs in the nearest town were scarce she'd secured part-time work at the local cinema. During the day she worked on the farm, and in the evenings she drove into town to sell tickets, usher in patrons, and dole out ice-cream and coffee before and after the shows.

And in between she sat at the back of the theatre and watched the larger-than-life characters on screen. The fantasy world of films was an antidote to the hard physical reality of the farm and the loneliness that went with it.

Watching in snatches, she'd seen some scenes over and over, missed others altogether, but become fascinated by the techniques of bringing a story to life. She hired videos, playing them again and again to study their structure, and borrowed books from the library about films and film-making.

One evening just before Shannon's nineteenth birthday her father didn't come in for his dinner, and in growing anxiety she went out into the gathering darkness and a fine Northland drizzle, eventually discovering his overturned tractor on a hillside, his twisted, mangled body beneath it.

The sale of the farm left very little money after mortgage payments had been taken care of, and she'd moved to Auckland where work was easier to find and opportunities less limited. She'd spent her meagre inheritance on a course in film-making, and after that had taken whatever jobs she could find in the industry, often working for nothing while she survived on an unemployment benefit. Then she'd begun to be offered paid positions, and over the next few years climbed the ladder to a job as second assistant director on a feature film before she met Devin.

It was a fluke meeting when they both became involved in a rush-hour mishap on the motorway. Shannon had been forced to take evasive action to avoid hitting a car that had spun out on the wet road in front of her, and as she changed lanes Devin's bumper clipped her rear, so that her car too went into a spin. She'd hit the median bar between opposing streams of traffic, careened back across the road—miraculously missing other cars that were screeching and ducking to avoid the original collision—and ended up facing the wrong way on the verge.

Devin drew up in front of her and leapt out, racing to open her door and demand, 'Are you hurt?'

Shaking, she said, 'No, I don't think so.'

He reached across to switch off her ignition and

unfasten her safety belt. 'Can you move? Be careful, and stop if anything hurts.'

Relieved, she'd found that nothing did.

Devin called the police and they both gave statements before Shannon's car was towed away. When it was all sorted and they'd exchanged cards for insurance purposes, Devin, whose Mercedes had got off lightly, said, 'Can I drive you somewhere?'

Still in a state of dazed shock, she said, 'Thank you. I have a meeting with a producer…' Then, glancing at her watch, added, 'I'll have to phone and ask if we can reschedule.'

After she'd done that he suggested a quiet cup of coffee. 'Or something stronger? I doubt if you're always as pale as you are now.'

She couldn't recall what they had talked about, only that his solid presence helped her jumping nerves, and his occasional dry humour, delivered with a grave face, made her laugh.

The cup of coffee had become two, then three, then lunch. Maybe because they were aware how near they had been to disaster, the normal social constraints dropped quickly away.

She felt she'd always known him.

When they parted Devin caught at her hand and said, 'May I phone you? And not about the insurance.'

'I'd like that,' she'd replied honestly, and smiled at him.

He didn't smile back. 'Thank you,' he said.

'I should be thanking you! You've been very kind, and given me a lot of your time.'

He laughed then. 'This isn't kindness, Shannon. It's sheer self-interest. Apart from the initial...impact, and the few seconds when I thought you might be injured, I haven't enjoyed myself so much in months. I'd like to see you again.'

He had, as often as they could snatch time together in the next few weeks, and behind his natural reserve she'd glimpsed a side of him that she later realised was seldom on view. Tenderness, warmth tinged with humour, and even raw passion. He was like no other man she'd ever met, the only one who could for a little time make her forget her burning ambition, put her single-minded passion for her work aside.

In less than two months he'd asked her to marry him, and she'd said yes without even thinking about it.

And then he'd taken her to meet his family.

Mrs Keynes appeared to have a deep-rooted distrust of anyone working in 'entertainment' with the possible exception of opera, ballet, and symphony orchestras. Her husband had progressed from disapproval to a slightly heavy-handed Dutch-uncle acceptance. Once he had confided that while Devin's stubborn streak could be damned inconvenient Ralph respected his son's strong will and determination. 'I see some of the same qualities in you,' he said, 'and Devin admires you for them...but watch out if you have a real difference of opinion. He doesn't like to be crossed.'

How true that was, she had soon discovered. And it didn't seem he had changed very much.

If she wasn't going to have sex with Devin, she could at least be scrupulous about keeping to the other terms of their agreement. So on Friday evening she dressed with care in a bias-cut black dress, hung a couple of fine gold chains around her neck, and swathed a gold mesh scarf about her shoulders, hoping she looked subdued enough to meet the Keynes' standards.

Marcia's greeting was superbly gracious, and Ralph kissed her cheek and squeezed her waist, apparently happy to see her.

Devin's sister, Lila, gave her a reserved smile, and her husband, a quiet, pleasant man named Payton Ellis who ran a modest import-export business, surprised Shannon with a brief hug as he said, 'Nice to see you again, Shannon. We've missed you.'

Perhaps he was glad to have an ally of sorts among the forceful Keynes clan.

Pre-dinner drinks were offered, and the atmosphere became less strained. During the meal Marcia and Lila inquired politely about Shannon's recent success, and Lila admitted to having seen *Heart of the Wilderness*. Her husband expanded enthusiastically on that, and Shannon was relieved to turn to him and listen to his comments.

Later, while Lila helped her mother serve coffee in the lounge, Ralph patted the sofa beside him and said, 'Shannon, come and talk to me.'

Shannon obeyed, conscious of Devin watching from across the room. Then Payton leaned over and engaged his attention as Lila handed coffee to her father and Shannon.

'So,' Ralph said, casting Shannon a frankly inquisitive look, 'you two are back together.'

She answered cautiously. 'We're…seeing how things go.'

'I hope they go well. My son needs someone like you.'

Startled, she said, 'You didn't think so at first.'

'I was concerned about the suddenness of it all. Out of character for Devin to be bowled over by a pretty face, but I could soon tell that you're much more than that.'

'He knows lots of prettier women than me.'

'Don't underestimate yourself, my dear—Devin knows quality when he sees it.' Reaching out to pat her hand, Ralph said, 'It's nice to have you back where you belong.'

'Thank you, but I don't think everyone feels…' She didn't finish the thought as her eyes went involuntarily to Ralph's wife and daughter, now seated side by side on another sofa.

'Don't worry about Marcia and Lila,' Ralph advised. 'If Devin wants you they'll come round. They're both very fond of him, you know. That's why they were angry with you for leaving him.'

She supposed they were. And if they had doubts about this apparent reconciliation she could hardly blame them. 'I don't think they ever liked me very much,' she murmured.

'They don't dislike you, Shannon!' Ralph chided. 'I think they were a little daunted by you.'

Shannon almost choked on a mouthful of coffee, putting the cup back in its saucer with a clatter. 'Daunted? How?'

'By your success in a field that's…well, rather exotic and glamorous, you know.'

'But they're…I mean, they have everything!'

'My wife,' Ralph said, 'is a clever woman who has devoted her life to her home and her family. I hope she has no regrets. Lila is doing very well in the business and I'll have no qualms about leaving it in her hands when I've had enough. But you know, working for the family firm, she's never had to struggle as you have.'

Bemused, Shannon glanced again at the two women. Was it possible their sophistication and poise hid secret insecurity? Ralph was no fool and he must know them both better than anybody.

Looking away, she found her gaze caught by Devin. He put down his cup, rose and strolled across to her and Ralph, perching himself on the sofa arm next to Shannon and laying a casual hand on her shoulder.

His father said, 'I hope you two are going to make it this time. Look after her, son.'

'I'm doing my best,' Devin replied. 'But I'm not sure that's what Shannon wants.'

'I don't need looking after,' she confirmed, an echo

of past arguments stirring in her mind. 'I'm not a child.'

Ralph patted her hand again. 'We can all do with a bit of pampering now and then,' he argued. 'Men as well as women.' He got up from his seat. 'Excuse me, my dear. Devin, you can sit with your wife.'

As Ralph walked over to talk to his son-in-law, Devin accepted the invitation and took his place, an arm draped over the back of the sofa. 'You and the old man having a tête-à-tête?' he asked. 'He has a soft spot for you.'

'I quite like him too.'

'Whenever you want to go,' Devin offered, 'just say the word.'

'It's your family party. I'll stay as long as you want.'

'Ah,' he said, 'that's what I've been waiting to hear.' A faint smile on his lips was the only sign he was teasing her.

She couldn't help a small answering smile, although it held a hint of scorn. 'You know what I meant.'

'Unfortunately, yes.' His hand left the sofa back and he lifted a strand of hair from her cheek, his warm fingers fleetingly brushing her skin and sending a tiny shiver of awareness through her. 'But I live in hope, Shannon. It's all I've got.'

His eyes had turned sombre, and she looked back at him uncertainly, caught unawares by his apparent sincerity. She reminded herself of her vow and turned away from temptation, presenting a deliberately aloof profile.

He said quietly, 'Let me know if you change your mind.'

Then his mother addressed some remark to him, and the conversation became general.

As they re-entered the apartment later Devin said, 'I appreciate the effort you made tonight.'

'It wasn't as difficult as I expected,' Shannon admitted. It hadn't been much to ask, after all.

'How about a nightcap?'

Shannon hesitated. 'All right.' He had been careful about his wine intake at dinner, knowing he was driving afterwards. Maybe he wanted company.

He gave her a liqueur and poured a whisky for himself. They hadn't switched on the centre light in the lounge, and a table lamp cast a muted glow.

Devin leaned back in his chair, watching her. 'Do you have a date yet for filming?'

'I plan to start at the end of the month.' There were several reasons for haste, not least the danger of someone stealing a march on her. 'And I hope we can wrap it up within four months.'

He glanced sharply at her. 'You said five or six.'

'We've found locations within the city area so we needn't travel far. It will help the budget too.' And she had condensed the time frame as much as she possibly could. The longer she stayed with Devin the harder it would be to leave him.

There was still a vital part to be cast, and not much time.

'Do you really think Rose would consider a part in it?'

'Maybe.' He grinned tauntingly. 'For me.'

Shannon unclenched her jaw and returned him a tight, bared-teeth smile. 'Nice for you to have friends in the right places.'

'I'm trying to be nice to *you*.'

A rebuke, and maybe she deserved it. She downed some more liqueur, burning her throat. 'I'm grateful,' she assured him. 'Truly.'

'Truly?' His eyes gleamed. Then, as hers met them and skittered away, he laughed. 'Don't worry, I don't want you coming to me out of gratitude, Shannon.'

'Then why are you doing this?'

'Like I said, I'm trying to help. That's what married people do, isn't it? Help each other?'

Shannon bit her lip. 'You never did before.'

He didn't answer immediately. 'You never needed it before.'

'I needed some…understanding.'

'Of your work?' he queried after a moment.

'Of what it means to me.'

'More than your marriage? Than our child?'

Shannon put down her glass and abruptly stood up. 'That's not fair.'

His voice roughened. 'If you hadn't insisted on working so damned hard you might not have lost the pregnancy.'

Her heart lurched sickeningly. The memory of that awful time haunted her. A raw wound that had never properly healed. 'There's no point in going over this again.' She turned away from him, trying to hide the pain that the subject aroused.

When she left the room he let her go, and didn't follow until after she'd fallen asleep, still fighting the memory of desolation, grief and despair. Of a time when she'd existed in some kind of vacuum, when Devin seemed distant and untouchable, even while they shared the same bed. When in a matter of a few months they'd grown so far apart that the final rift had merely confirmed their isolation from each other.

She woke with an insistent throbbing at her temples. Devin's side of the bed looked untouched and she could hear no sound. Entering the living area after dressing, she saw no sign of him. He must have left for work early.

The whisky bottle sat on the coffee table, empty alongside his glass. Maybe she wasn't the only one with a headache.

The night before he flew to America, Devin stayed late at the office. Shannon was working too, in the room she'd converted into an office-workroom, and didn't hear him come in.

When he opened the door of the room she swung round with wide, startled eyes, and he said, 'I didn't mean to frighten you. I thought perhaps you'd gone to bed without turning off the light.'

Shannon glanced at her watch. 'I hadn't thought about the time.' She was standing at the table, a collection of sketches almost covering it. Turning back to them, she put down her pencil and absently wedged her hands into the small of her aching back, arching it.

Devin walked forward and she felt his hands on her shoulders, massaging them, his fingers strong and intimate.

His touch electrified her, momentarily halting her breath.

But she didn't want him to stop. Dipping her head, she forced herself to breathe normally, her fingertips touching the table before her.

Looking over her shoulder, he said, 'What are you doing?'

'A storyboard. It helps me visualise the scenes and show the crew how I see them being played.'

'You plan every move beforehand?'

'More or less. But everything is flexible. The art director and the DOP will have some input too. Even the actors.'

'DOP?'

'Director of Photography.'

'Oh, yes.' He stopped massaging but she was conscious of the warmth of his body behind her. His breath stirred her hair, then fanned her cheek as he leaned forward to study what she'd done. 'I never realised how much was involved.'

'You weren't interested.' He had been at first, in a

slightly puzzled fashion, but the interest soon waned. 'You thought it was a frivolous occupation.'

'You think I didn't respect your work?' He shifted his grip, turning her to face him.

Shannon gazed back at him mutely. She wasn't about to contradict him.

He said, 'I know you're good at what you do. I just couldn't share or condone your obsession with it, and in the end it came between us, so by then…I'd begun to hate it.'

'Hating my work is hating a part of me!' Her work involved her heart and soul as well as mind and body, but he had never understood that, never made the effort to do so.

'It wasn't you I hated!' he said with controlled force. Something leapt in his eyes, a dark flame. 'I *loved* you with every atom of my being. But that was never enough for you.'

Loved? She noted the past tense, her heart plunging. Her gaze swept his face, trying to decipher his expression. She saw desire there, and a fiercely controlled anger that stopped her breath.

His hands gripped her shoulders, and she realised there were only inches between them. He closed that small gap and bent his head to her, so that her eyelids involuntarily drifted shut as his mouth wreaked its magic on hers.

His lips were warm and compelling, his hold tightening as he moved one hand to her waist and deepened the kiss, making her head tip further back. He opened her mouth to him, and she found herself clutching at the sleeves of his jacket. She felt the strength of his arms, the hardness of his body, the heat that scorched through her clothing. He laid a hand against her breast and fire raced along her veins.

When at last his lips left hers he pressed them to the side of her neck and muttered, 'Come to bed, Shannon.'

Terribly tempted, for a moment she remained locked against him, but then a familiar fear and distrust intruded and she pushed her hands at his chest in rejection. The table behind her preventing her from moving, she said sharply, 'Let go, Devin!'

He lifted his head, and she saw a dazed expression in his eyes, then a flicker of what might have been chagrin. Stepping back, he released her so suddenly that instinctively she clutched the edge of the table behind her for support.

'Cutting off your nose to spite your face?' he asked with savage mockery. 'Or to spite me.'

'It isn't spite.' It was self-preservation. Self-respect.

'What, then? Pride? A way of punishing me…and yourself?'

'What if I am? Isn't that what this is all about?'

He frowned. 'What do you mean by that?'

'This whole…charade. Pretending to be reconciled. What you're really doing is punishing *me* for leaving you. Asserting your dominance in our relationship.'

He looked briefly nonplussed, almost shocked, so

that she couldn't help a twinge of doubt. Harshly he said, 'Is that what you truly believe?'

'If you were really interested in repairing our marriage,' she accused, 'you wouldn't have waited until I gave you the chance to force me into coming back to you.'

She'd been so close to giving in it frightened her. The surest form of defence was attack. Wildly she lashed out. 'You want me to give in and prove you can do whatever you want with me…. Well, it isn't going to happen. Nothing will make me have sex with you again!'

'Nothing?' He had folded his arms, looking at her with derision and slowly smouldering anger. 'You should know better than to throw out challenges to me, Shannon. Let's see if you can live up to your brave little speech.'

Before she could stop him he had reached for her again, catching her wrist, and even as she tried to wrest it away he had pulled her against him, then lifted her into his powerful arms.

CHAPTER SIX

'WHAT are you doing?' Shannon gasped, her heart thundering in fright, because he looked grim and determined and his hold was inescapable.

'Taking you to bed,' Devin said.

'You can't! You prom—'

He silenced her with a hard, passionate kiss, sending hot lightning bolts of sensation through her. Dimly she was aware that they had left the living room, and then he was shouldering open the bedroom door.

He dumped her on the bed and threw off his jacket, and when she tried to sit up his body came down on top of hers, pressing her against the pillows, her wrists held in implacable hands, his mouth wreaking a kind of depredation on hers.

She opened her mouth to bite him, and he drew back with a harsh laugh, then his lips were on her throat, her shoulder, and she felt his teeth on her skin, not hurting but an erotic warning.

He kissed her again, fleetingly, allowing her no time to retaliate, and his thigh pushed between hers while his mouth was exploring the sensitive spot just below her ear, and she felt the slight, sexy rasp of his tongue.

Her heart pounded suffocatingly, her body consumed by licks of fire. 'Devin,' she said, her voice nothing but a breathless moan. 'Don't do this. *Don't.*'

His thigh moved insidiously against hers, setting up a delicious friction, that made her sink her teeth into her lower lip in the effort not to reciprocate.

'Stop fighting it,' he said. 'Stop fighting *me,* my darling. You've no need to be afraid.'

'I do, if you're going to force me.' But the tenderness in his voice was almost too much.

'I won't need to force you,' he said, his hand freeing one of hers to go to the opening of the blouse she wore with her jeans. 'Let go, Shannon, let it happen. You know you want to.'

His fingers dealt deftly with two buttons before she caught at his hand to stop him.

She should have used the momentary freedom to hit him. He curled his fingers about hers and lifted her hand, taking the tip of one finger into his mouth, holding it between his teeth while his tongue teased the pad.

'Stop it!' she choked out.

He removed her finger from his mouth, but didn't let go her hand, instead pressing it against his heart's rapid beat. 'Feel that,' he said. 'Feel what you do to me.' He moved his lower body, and she knew he was completely aroused, the knowledge increasing her own reluctant arousal.

'I don't care!' She struggled to contain her own desire. 'I don't *want* you! I don't want to make love with you.'

'Liar.' His tone was amused. He shifted down a bit and she felt the heat of his lips on the swell of flesh above the minuscule cups of her bra. He brought their joined hands to it, pushing aside the lace, touching her, then turned her hand so that she could feel her own response. 'Can you deny what this is telling me?'

The sexual charge was overwhelming. Her whole body shuddered with it. She cried out in despair, a final, frantic plea before she was rushed into the whirlwind. 'No! Devin...don't make me hate you!'

'Hate me?' Devin stilled, seemed to stop breathing. 'This doesn't feel like hate, Shannon.'

'Whatever it feels like to you,' she told him, 'it isn't love. You think if you don't physically hurt me, if you make me want you in the end, then it's all right. But it isn't.' She drew in a shaking breath. 'Go ahead then, if that's what you really want. If you don't care about me as a person, only as an object you can use. I know you can make me respond, kiss you back, touch you, even beg for your touch in return. You'll give me pleasure that I've never known since I left you, you'll make sure I'm physically satisfied. I might even fall asleep in your arms. But I promise you,' she finished with conviction, 'in the morning I'll hate you. Even worse, I'll hate myself.'

She realised with horror that she was crying, and although she loathed and despised tears she was unable to stop them. They dripped down into her hair and onto the pillow.

'Maybe I'm desperate enough to take that risk,' he said harshly, and lowered his head.

Shannon braced herself, determined to deny him any response, even though she knew resistance was futile. But as his lips found her tear-wet cheek he went suddenly still, and let out a muffled, explosive word.

In the darkness she couldn't see Devin's face, only the outline of him looming over her. She drew in an unsteady breath, and the next instant she was free, the weight of his body removed as he flung himself on his back beside her, then left the bed altogether.

'You win,' he said. 'Or we both lose. Cry yourself to sleep if you want, I'll be spending the night in the spare room.'

His shadowy form disappeared and she heard the door close behind him. For a moment she lay motionless, then she turned and buried her head in the pillow, angrily trying to stem the silent tears soaking into the linen.

Shannon woke to daylight and a heavy, thumping headache. Everything was quiet except for the distant hum of traffic in the streets below. She used the bathroom and dressed, and when she emerged into the passageway saw the door of the guest room was open, the bed neatly made up.

She found Devin in the kitchen drinking coffee, unshaven and looking as though he'd slept in his clothes. If he'd slept at all. His eyes were shadowed and the taut skin over his cheekbones colourless.

When he saw her he put down his coffee cup with a thud and pushed his chair back, making it rock as he stood up with unusual clumsiness. 'Shannon,' he said. 'Are you all right?'

'Yes.'

She crossed to the bread container, took two slices from a packet and dropped them into the toaster.

'I'm sorry,' he said without moving, 'about last night.'

Her shoulders stiffened. 'Hadn't you better get away? Your plane leaves at ten, doesn't it?'

There was a short pause, then she heard him leave the room, and relaxed a little. The toast popped up, perfectly browned. All his appliances worked exactly the way they should. She took out the two slices, looked at them, and threw them into the stainless-steel bin. The thought of eating made her feel sick.

She was sitting at the table staring at a cup of cooling coffee when Devin reappeared, shaved and suited and carrying a large briefcase. 'I have to go,' he said, casting a frowning glance at the stainless-steel watch on his wrist. 'You will be here when I come home?'

Her mouth twisted. 'I don't have a choice, do I? Or I risk you pulling the plug on the film.' Even if she could bring herself to give up on it, so many other people were relying on it for their immediate income and future career paths, her name in the industry would be mud.

'I have the script,' Devin said, 'for Rose.'

She looked up. 'Good.' A foolish reply, but she couldn't say any more. Her gaze dropped.

He remained there a few more seconds, perhaps waiting for her to look at him again. Then he turned away.

She heard the front door close, then let her head drop into her hands, her thumbs kneading at her temples.

How long could they go on this way?

Despite her relief that she didn't have to face him every day after that fraught episode, she missed Devin more than she had expected—the evening talks over a drink, the occasional laughter, the times they'd shared preparing a meal and then eating together—even the sound of his quiet breathing in the bed beside her, and the hiss of the shower when he got up in the morning.

The apartment seemed very big and very empty. She ate out the first night with friends, and the following evenings snacked while she worked.

On Friday she had a meeting with the casting director, arranging auditions for some minor parts and discussing more possibles for the fiancée, because if the slim chance of getting Rose Grady fell through, they'd need to fill the gap quickly.

On her way out of the building she almost collided with Craig.

'Shannon!' He gave her a hug and kissed her cheek. 'Have you got time for a coffee?'

'I want to get back, there might be messages on the

answer machine. Why don't you come round and we can have a coffee at…my place?' She could do with some comfortable company.

In the apartment she handed him the latest copy of the script to read while she made the coffee and a snack, and they were still poring over the script a couple of hours on when Devin walked in.

He stopped in the doorway, his briefcase in one hand, a bag over his shoulder. He looked handsome and a little tired, and decidedly grim.

'Devin!' Shannon said. 'I wasn't expecting you today.'

'I finished my business earlier than I thought I would.'

His eyes flicked from her to Craig and she stood up, saying, 'You remember Craig, don't you?'

'Vividly.'

Craig shot a glance at Shannon's confused expression and stood up too, shoulder to shoulder with her. He half lifted a protective arm at her back, then dropped it without touching her. 'I'm flattered.'

Shannon rushed into speech. 'We were just going over the latest script changes.' Mentally she kicked herself for making excuses. She had no need to justify inviting a friend and colleague round. Hadn't Devin said this was her home?

'I see,' he said evenly. 'If you'll excuse me, I just got off a long flight. I'd like to freshen up.'

As Devin left the room, Craig said, 'Should I go?'

'Certainly not. Sit down. Would you like another coffee? Or something else?'

'I could do with a whisky after that...er... interruption,' he said, 'if you have some.'

They did, and she poured herself a glass of wine, resuming her seat beside him.

Devin came back into the room, having changed into casual cotton trousers and a loose sand-coloured shirt.

'Do you want a drink?' Shannon asked him. 'Or something to eat?'

Crossing to the drinks cabinet, he said shortly, 'I'll get my own drink.'

Apparently not interested in eating, he sat leaning against the back of the other couch and regarding them with a closed, unreadable expression.

Shannon said, 'How was the trip?'

Devin shrugged. 'Fine.'

'Did you...' She faltered, wondering if he'd thought about his promise.

'Rose is reading the script.' He was looking strangely unapproachable, holding a shot glass in one hand, the other arm flung over the back of the couch that he had all to himself.

'Thank you.' Shannon explained to Craig, 'Devin knows Rose Grady. He took her a copy of the script.'

'Wow!' Craig gazed at Devin with new respect. Turning to Shannon again, he said, 'She'd be wonderful as the fiancée. Um...you don't have a Hollywood star in mind for the witness, do you?'

She touched his hand. 'You know I want you, Craig.'

He grinned with obvious relief. 'I'd love to work with Rose.'

'Don't count on it, she probably wouldn't be free even if she's interested.' Maybe she was only reading the script—or pretending to—as a favour to her old 'friend.'

Craig said, 'I'll cross my fingers.'

'I'd be a bit nervous about directing her,' Shannon confessed.

'You're a damn good director. Remember you're the one in charge.'

'Thank you.' She smiled at him gratefully. It was nice to praised by an actor.

Devin put down his glass, the sound making Shannon start guiltily. He had been left out of the conversation, not only because Craig was her guest, but because she couldn't forget the constraint of the morning of Devin's departure, and the drama of the night before.

Craig glanced at him and finished his own drink. 'Well, I'll leave you to it. Thanks, Shannon. You'll let me know when you need me?'

She walked him to the door and closed it behind him, then went slowly back to the living room. Devin had left his chair and was getting himself another drink.

'How did your business go?' she asked him when he turned.

'I thought you'd never ask.'

'I didn't know if you'd want to talk about it in front of Craig.'

He looked as though he might not believe her, but as she hesitated he said, 'Sit down. You're like a nervous deer, hovering over there.'

'I'm not nervous.' She sat down again to prove it, and was disconcerted when he strolled over to sit on the same couch, although leaving a good couple of feet of space between them. He propped an elbow on the back of it and scanned her face. 'My business was successful,' he said. 'But I don't want to spend so much time away now that...there's someone to come home to.'

That was her. Unexpectedly, she had to swallow a lump in her throat, a clutch of longing.

She said, 'I'm really grateful to you for getting Rose to read the script.'

'How grateful?' he asked softly, his eyes questioning her.

She looked away. 'I've moved my things into the spare room,' she said baldly. 'I hope you won't object.'

There was a taut silence. Then he said, his tone hardening, 'Fair enough. Admittedly I broke our agreement. I suppose an apology isn't sufficient to change your mind? Because I certainly owe you one.'

Shannon shook her head. She had been much too close to breaking her own resolution that night. She couldn't trust herself if anything like that happened again.

'You always were a stubborn woman.' He shifted his position and she tensed, but he only leaned back, looking up for a moment at the ceiling.

She dared a small, slightly shaky laugh. 'You can talk.'

Devin turned his head to look at her, answering humour gleaming under half-closed lids. 'I don't give up easily, true. So be warned, sweetheart.'

The word was a mockery, yet it turned her heart to mush. She wanted to be in his arms, snuggling against him the way she used to in the early days of their marriage, before it all went so horribly wrong. Rallying her defences, she said, 'Does that mean I can expect more caveman tactics?'

'I thought I'd made it clear you were safe. You always were. Do you think I don't know what you were fighting that night? Not me, was it?'

'Whatever your ego decides.'

He laughed, not kindly. 'Keep your pride then. It won't be much company in your lonely bed.'

'If you don't mind,' she said, 'I'll go to it now. I've had a tiring day.' She got up, then paused, noting the fine lines about his eyes and the hollows below his cheekbones. He must be tired too, and maybe jet-lagged. 'Are you sure I can't get you something first?'

'Spoken like a good little wife,' he said, lifting his glass in an ironic toast, and then tossing off the remaining whisky. 'But the only thing I want at the moment is the one thing you won't offer me. I'd give a lot for a warm, willing woman in my arms right now.' He looked at her fully, his eyes challenging, his mouth taking on a sardonic quirk.

Oh, he was temptation incarnate. She stiffened her spine and said, 'Sorry. I'm not available.'

'I didn't think so.' He continued to study her, and she shook herself mentally and moved away from his hypnotic gaze.

Part of her wanted to throw her scruples to the wind and take what he offered, give him what he needed. But every time she remembered how he'd got her here in his home her spirit rebelled and something froze around her heart. All she had to hang on to was the remnant of her pride.

The weekend came and Devin said, 'Why don't we have a night out?' At her surprised look he expanded, 'Just the two of us. We could take in a film, have a meal afterwards.' He paused, and in a carefully neutral tone added, 'Or are you too busy?'

'No,' she admitted. Soon she wouldn't have time for a social life, but if he wanted her company tonight she could put off the work she'd planned and do as he asked.

'Then what would you like to see…do?'

'Films aren't your favourite entertainment.' He had never shared her enthusiasm.

'I don't have your specialist knowledge,' he said,

'but that doesn't stop me enjoying a good movie. You can educate me.'

'Educate you?'

'You're the expert.'

'And you want to learn?'

'Yes,' he said. 'Yes, I do. You choose which film, and I'll pick a restaurant.'

In the darkened theatre Shannon found it difficult to concentrate. She had taken off the jacket she wore over a sleeveless dress, and her bare arm brushed against Devin's shirt-sleeved one, setting up a tingling awareness. When she covertly glanced at him she could see his strong profile silhouetted in the dim light, reminding her of the many times they had shared a more intimate darkness in the bed they used to sleep in, make love in. She could even smell his subtle male body scent and a faint whiff of his aftershave.

Resolutely she turned her attention to the screen, where the characters were acting out a complicated drama involving a number of shifting relationships.

Making their way out of the theatre, she felt the light touch of Devin's hand on her waist as though it were capable of burning her flesh through the thin fabric of her dress.

In the restaurant Devin wanted to know, 'So what did you think?'

'Tell me what you thought first,' she countered.

'An amateur opinion? I could be setting myself up to be shot down in flames.'

'I'm not setting you up,' she denied. 'After all, you're the target audience, the ordinary viewer who just wants to see a good film and enjoy a night out. Your opinion counts.'

He shrugged. 'It was well acted and the photography was superb. The story was kind of interesting but it seemed artificial to me.'

'A good plot shouldn't appear contrived. You couldn't believe in it?'

'No.' He reached for a glass of wine, resting his fork for a moment. 'Did you?'

'While I was watching, yes. Unlikely, but then plenty of true stories are even more unbelievable.'

He asked curiously, 'If you find true stories unbelievable, how can you believe in something made up?'

'The events may be made up, but they can illustrate a truth about life, emotions…people.'

'Illuminate the human condition?' He laughed. 'I've never figured that one out. Is there such a thing, when every human being is different from every other one?'

A woman with a basket of flowers for sale entered the restaurant, and Devin called her over, chose a red rose and presented it to Shannon.

She took it hesitantly. 'Thank you, but you didn't need to…'

His eyes sombre, he said, 'I thought about buying you flowers on my way home from the airport, but it seemed…inadequate.'

She looked down, laying the rose on the tablecloth. 'This is lovely,' she said.

When they returned to the apartment she looked for something to put it in, settling for a champagne flute after cutting the stem of the flower so it would fit.

Devin lingered, watching her. She placed the rose on the dining table and turned to find him lounging in the doorway. She said, 'I…enjoyed tonight.'

There had been a kind of bitter-sweetness about the evening, recalling earlier times.

'We should do it again.'

Shannon nodded. But they could never return to those uncomplicated days early in their marriage. Too much had come between them since then.

Shannon was into frenzied pre-production mode. She'd hired an assistant producer, but overall the project was hers and she wanted everything to be as perfect as possible.

On her birthday Devin suggested an early dinner and a visit to the opera at the Aotea Centre. He knew she loved the richness of the costumes and sets as well as the drama of the acting and music. 'You can dress up,' he said, 'wear something glamorous.'

And do him justice, Shannon thought cynically, then smothered the unworthy thought.

She dressed in a slim-fitting ruby-red chiffon dress, ruched over satin, with tiny black beads sewn into the folds, winking in the light, and flung a black lace exotically bead-fringed shawl over her shoulders.

Devin, handsome in black tie and jacket, surveyed her with approval when she joined him in the living room. 'You look wonderful,' he said, his eyes kindling.

'Thank you.' She busied herself adjusting the wrap, avoiding the danger of meeting his gaze.

'I hope this will go with it,' he said, and handed her a package wrapped in gift paper.

'I wasn't expecting a present.'

'It's your birthday. Of course you get a present.'

'But you're taking me to the opera.'

'Open it.'

Reluctantly she peeled back the gift wrapping, revealing a jeweller's box.

The bracelet nestled against white satin was exquisite, a circle of twisted gold threads set with deep red stones.

'Rubies?' she asked with trepidation. It must have cost a fortune.

'Garnets,' Devin said. 'Are you disappointed?'

'No! This is beautiful, but I can't take it, Devin.'

'Of course you can take it.' His voice held a harsh note. 'You're my wife and I want you to have it. No strings,' he added. 'I'm not trying to bribe you into bed with me, Shannon, if that's what you're thinking.'

'I wasn't,' she protested.

'Then say thank you nicely and put it on.'

'I...well, thank you.' She looked down at the gorgeous thing, unable to suppress a pang of guilt. It was an extravagant present for a wife who refused to be one in the fullest sense. 'Thank you very much.'

He lifted it from its nest of satin. 'Here, let me.'

Mutely she allowed him to fasten the bracelet about her wrist. He captured her hand, turning it so the bracelet slipped a little, the stones glittering under the overhead light. Then he dropped a light kiss on her palm, making it tingle. 'I hope that isn't a breach of contract,' he said, releasing her. 'Come on, we don't want to be late.'

The opera was a sumptuous feast of sound and sight, and Shannon managed to lose herself in its extravagance, emerging into the cool night air afterwards feeling euphoric and almost dazed.

'That was wonderful,' she said as Devin took her arm to guide her through the departing crowd.

'One of the best I've seen,' he agreed.

Curious, she asked, 'If you think films are unbelievable, what about opera? Their plots are really out of this world.'

Devin laughed. 'I just enjoy the music. There's no requirement to accept the silly story.'

A hearty male voice hailed Devin and a big hand clapped his shoulder. 'Hey, Dev! How's tricks? Haven't seen you in a while.'

Devin's hand on Shannon's arm halted her. He turned to the burly, balding man and the small blond woman clinging to his arm. 'Shannon, you remember Con and Amy, don't you?'

Two pairs of astonished eyes regarded her before both faces broke into smiles. Con boomed, 'Shannon, sweetheart! So you two are back together? That's great.' He leaned down and kissed her cheek as his wife was saying warmly, 'It's nice to see you again, Shannon.'

She couldn't help being touched at their genuine pleasure. Con was an old schoolmate of Devin's and she had liked the couple best of all his friends, but she hadn't seen them since the break-up.

'This calls for a celebration,' Con decided. 'Let's find a bar.' He led the way and found them a table, insisting on ordering a bottle of sparkling wine, though after one glass Devin settled for coffee.

'We saw *Heart of the Wilderness*,' Amy told her. 'It was great. I've been telling everyone I know the director.'

'Name-dropper,' her husband teased amiably, pouring himself more bubbly and refilling Shannon's glass. 'Now Shannon's back,' he said to Devin, 'maybe you'll be less like a cat on hot bricks and stop flitting about the world so much. You've been flamin' hard to pin down ever since the split.'

'I do have business interests in Australia and America,' Devin said mildly.

Con made a scornful sound. 'Well, when can the two of you come to dinner? We've got a lot to catch up on.'

Amy said, 'Yes, we must get together. Maybe one night next week? I'll phone you.'

Devin put down the spoon he'd been stirring his coffee with. 'I don't know if Shannon can spare the time.'

Shannon scarcely hesitated. 'I'm sure we can work out a date,' she said quickly. 'I'll look forward to it, Amy.'

She would make the time, she promised herself, determined to fulfil her agreement with Devin. Besides, she too would enjoy an evening with the couple, even if the timing was less than ideal.

'What are you doing now, Shannon?' Con asked. 'Got another film in the works?'

'A full-length feature,' she said.

'It's a Victorian mystery,' Devin interposed.

Shannon listened in surprise as he described the script succinctly but with obvious, if restrained, enthusiasm.

Con asked, 'When will we be able to see it?'

'We start shooting soon,' Shannon told him. The production manager and art director were frantically hunting through antique and junk shops for period furnishings, and the wardrobe department was already working overtime.

'Shannon's in a hurry to get it finished,' Devin said dryly, casting her a glance that made her flush.

She said, 'It will be next year before it's released.' And reached for her coffee.

Amy said, 'What a lovely bracelet.'

'It's her birthday present,' Devin said.

'Gorgeous!' Amy said enviously. 'Happy Birthday. Devin has very good taste.'

'You betcha.' Con chuckled. 'Can't understand why he let this woman slip through his fingers.' Turning to his friend, he added, 'Better hold on to her this time, mate.'

'I intend to.' Devin's voice was perfectly level. Shannon didn't dare look at him.

The after-effect of the music, the wine, the company of people she'd forgotten she liked so much, and Devin's manner—that of a devoted husband—threatened her resolve not to lose sight of the reality. On the way home she found herself fighting a curious mixture of poignant memories and simmering resentment.

Once there, Devin said, 'Join me in a nightcap?'

An order, or an invitation? She sat on the edge of a couch and watched as he poured brandy into snifters.

'Thank you,' he said, handing one to her.

'Isn't that my line? Why should you thank me?'

'I thought you might not want to have dinner with my friends.'

Nervous and unsettled, she said, 'You've no need to thank me for fulfilling my obligations.'

For an instant the hand lifting the glass to his mouth stilled, before he completed the movement and swallowed some brandy. 'Obligations?' he queried softly.

'Under our agreement.'

He looked away, seemingly gazing at nothing for a second or two, then his eyes homed in on hers. 'Why do you need to remind me, Shannon? Or yourself?'

He was right, but she said, 'I don't have to remind myself that I'm here under duress, Devin.'

'So why spoil a pleasant evening?'

'I'm sorry.' Perhaps she was being mean-spirited. The birthday treat had been an attempt to soften things for her, but it didn't change the stark facts. 'I just can't forget that…this whole situation is artificial. And I don't know exactly what you hope to gain by it.'

'The only thing artificial about it is your determination to keep me at arm's length.'

'I don't agree.'

He laughed shortly and finished his drink. 'Well, we'll see how long it will last.'

Was he so confident of her eventual surrender? Did he realise how humiliating it would be for her if she succumbed? She was haunted by the fear that he wanted to see her humbled, her pride in tatters.

Suppose she gave in, and he threw her aside afterwards, having gained his point, and a sweet revenge?

'Thank you for my birthday treat,' she said huskily, standing up. 'I had a lovely evening.'

Devin stood up too, but didn't make a move toward her. 'I'm glad,' he said, and when she left the room he was still where she had left him, looking after her with enigmatic eyes.

CHAPTER SEVEN

DINNER with Amy and Con was relaxing and fun. Con had a way of making Devin seem more open, younger. Shannon supposed Devin could let down his guard with his old schoolmate.

Amy cheerfully allowed her guests to help her serve mouth-watering dishes and clear up afterwards. There was another couple too, the woman a children's book illustrator and the man a painter who specialised in big, splashy acrylic works for public buildings.

Devin seemed to get on well with both of them, listening intently to the painter's description of techniques, questioning him about the theory of abstract and surreal art.

At the end of the evening Devin said, 'You must all come and have dinner with us. Shannon?'

'We'll arrange a date,' she promised.

In the car he said, 'I hope you're not annoyed at me asking them without consulting you first.'

'I'll look forward to seeing them again.'

'They might enjoy meeting some of *your* friends.'

'My friends?' She blinked at him.

Before, when she had entertained her film-world friends he'd been courteous but aloof. Once or twice she'd detected a tremor of quickly hidden astonish-

ment when he was confronted with a particularly striking example of dress sense, or a hair-raising account
of some personal adventure in the trade or out of it.

Deducing that Devin disapproved of her flamboyant
companions, Shannon had gradually taken to seeing
them elsewhere than the home she shared with him.

At the apartment when Shannon turned toward her
bedroom, Devin said, 'Don't go yet.'

'What do you want?'

'You seemed to be having a good time tonight.'

'Con and Amy were always fun. And they accepted
me from the first. Not like—'

'Like…?' he queried.

'Most of your friends couldn't understand why you
married me.' She looked away from him, a sad smile
curling her lips. 'Well, neither could I.'

'I married you because I was in love with you!
Blindly, insanely in love.'

The words he'd used were a dead giveaway. Like
her, he'd been caught up in an attraction so powerful
that their differences in background, in careers and
lifestyle and long-term goals, seemed mere trifles to
be swept away by the sheer force of their mutual desire. His family's reservations and the surprise of his
friends and business associates had apparently passed
him by. He had eyes only for her.

'Both of us were insane,' she acknowledged.

'You were keen enough at the time.'

She had been. 'It was nice while it lasted.'

'*Nice?*' He laughed. 'That isn't how I would have described it.'

'I'm sorry if I disappointed you.'

He looked irritated. 'You were never a disappointment, Shannon. Maddening, exhilarating, stubborn, provocative—but never a disappointment.'

'I couldn't be the corporate wife you needed.'

'I never expected that of you.'

'No?' she queried sceptically. 'Everyone else did.'

'Who the hell cares about everyone else?'

'You did. You wanted me by your side at all the dinners and business functions, making small talk and being charming and polite.'

'I wanted you by my side,' he agreed, 'because I missed you when you weren't there, and because I was proud of you, proud that I was your husband, that you'd chosen to spend your life with me—as I thought then.'

'I thought I would,' she said, around the lump in her throat. 'I intended to, you know that.'

'How could I? I have no idea what was in your mind when you married me.'

Her mind hadn't had a lot to do with it. Her heart, her body, had been so dazzled by him that her brain had gone into hibernation. 'We should have known it would never work out.'

'It might have if you'd been willing to try a bit harder.'

'If *I'd* been willing?' Her head jerked up. 'There were two of us in that marriage, Devin.'

'*This* marriage,' he emphasised. 'It isn't over yet.'

'There's no going back.'

'We could try going forward…together.'

'I…' Doubt warred with an insidious hope. Was he serious about giving their marriage another chance? Could there be more than damaged pride and a desire to salvage it behind his outrageous terms?

'I know I coerced you into this,' he said, 'and maybe that was a mistake, but I'd like us to try again.'

'Why?' she asked, suspicious and wary.

'Maybe,' he said slowly, 'because I don't like to admit failure. Because I believe our marriage deserves another chance.'

She studied him doubtfully.

He allowed a spasm of exasperation to cross his face. 'You seem convinced I have some kind of power complex, that I want you on your knees. For God's sake, Shannon, do you really believe I'm that vindictive?'

Maybe she'd been unfair, mistaken. 'No,' she said slowly. 'I guess not.' Their marriage hadn't lasted long enough for real intimacy on other than a sexual level. She hadn't known him well enough to be certain of his motives.

'Then give it a chance, Shannon. I won't pressure you, but we had something good for a little while. We can make it good again.'

He walked toward her and his palms shaped her shoulders. 'What do we have to lose?'

He was so persuasive in this mood. So…reasonable.

As he had been when he'd first tried to talk her into throwing in her job, insisting she had no need to work, he could look after her every need.

He'd been perplexed at her refusal, laughing a little at her determined independence. Only later, as she continued to stick to her resolve despite her pregnancy, he'd become increasingly cold and implacable.

If that happened again she had a *lot* to lose. She wouldn't, she had sworn, be pushed into the same dilemma again, forced to choose between her career and her marriage. It had been agonising and she didn't think she could stand a repetition.

Excuses crowded her mind, born of a deep and paralysing inner panic. She was unable to cope with the implications. 'I can't deal with this now,' she said, drawing away from him. 'While I'm involved in the film I don't have the energy to become embroiled in a relationship.'

He stepped back, releasing her. A chillingly familiar anger hardened his voice. 'I see. You still put your work above all else.'

'That's what you couldn't stand, wasn't it?' she flashed at him. 'That I wouldn't be the little woman sitting at home and waiting on her lord and master's pleasure.'

'I simply couldn't see that filming needed to consume every waking moment, especially when you were pregnant!'

When they met she had just finished working on a film and was hoping for another, filling in with casual jobs that left her free to be with him almost anytime. Then she landed an assistant director's place and Devin had suddenly found her chronically unavailable.

'I warned you how it would be,' she reminded him now. She'd explained that filming was often weeks and months of frantic activity followed by a lull, and he'd accepted that. 'I had no choice.'

She'd missed him and felt guilty, but she was determined to make the best of the opportunity.

'You had choices,' Devin argued. 'You chose your career over our marriage.'

'It wasn't as simple as that!' She had, in fact, spent months juggling them.

'Forgive me,' he said with an edge of sarcasm that made her bristle, 'but to me it looked exactly like that.'

'You don't understand. You never really wanted to.'

Anxious to do well despite a project beset with problems and personality clashes, and a difficult director, she'd been stressed and tired. Devin became impatient, and when she'd unexpectedly got pregnant he had decreed with increasing insistence that she ought to work less, rest more, even give up altogether and let him look after her. He could well afford it.

They had argued about her early morning starts and long days, but having longed for this opportunity to show her skills she was determined to carry it through.

And then she lost the baby and everything turned to dust.

Devin drew in an audible breath. '*You* didn't seem to care that you were endangering your health, and the baby's! What was I supposed to do? Stand by and let you do it?'

Stricken, she was silent, and he reached out a hand to her.

'God, Shannon! I didn't mean to hurt you.'

She pulled away. 'You were jealous.'

He made a dismissive gesture. 'Maybe that was part of it, at first. I'd have dealt with that if you hadn't been growing thinner, developing hollows under your eyes, obviously driving yourself too hard.'

'I could have done with some support,' she cried, 'instead of bullying!'

'Bullying?' Unusually, emotion was raw in his face. Shock and fury whitened his cheeks. 'I was trying to protect you!'

She supposed he had been, but it had only added extra pressure to those she already felt. 'It didn't help,' she said bitterly.

He shook his head. 'I don't know what else I could have done.'

The telephone rang, he glanced irritably at his watch and strode over to answer it, barking his name into the receiver.

Gathering it was a business call from overseas, Shannon seized the chance to escape. By the time the murmur of his voice ceased she'd switched off her light.

Early the following morning the phone rang again, waking Shannon from an erotic dream in which Devin figured vividly. They were lying in tall, waving grasses, and she could hear the sea nearby. Devin was touching her, tickling her cheek, her neck, between her breasts, with the silky head of a grass stem. They were in swimsuits, and his bare chest gleamed with salt water. She took the grass from his hand and ran it across his skin, and he laughed down at her, then bent to her and kissed her breasts, above the minimal bikini top she wore. Looking up at a blue, blue sky, she sighed, closed her eyes, and then miraculously there was nothing between her and Devin, only cool water slicking their skins as they came together and she arched her back against his hand, her body shaped to his, his mouth claiming hers.

A mixture of memory and fantasy, she realised, struggling awake to the shrill, insistent interruption. The grass and the nearby sea existed, and they had once made love there, but not without struggling out of wet, sandy swimsuits amid laughter and her not very convincing protests. Devin had turned so she lay on him, his hard-muscled body shielding her from the harsh grass and sand, and afterwards he'd sworn he felt no discomfort and she'd teased that he was too macho to admit to it.

'No,' he said. 'You were so beautiful, all I felt was your lovely body against me and your sweet heat when I was inside you.'

His bedroom door opened, then there was silence.

Shannon, sleeping in a skimpy short nightdress, reached for her cream satin robe as she headed for her own door. Light spilled into the passageway from the kitchen and she followed it, finding Devin, clad only in black shorts, making himself coffee. The kitchen clock said it was four-thirty.

Devin turned as she said, 'Is anything wrong? I heard the phone.' Even his overseas calls didn't usually come through at this hour.

He pushed a hand over his sleep-tousled hair and smiled at her, a spark lighting his eyes as he took in her attire. 'Nothing,' he said. 'Rose got the time difference wrong between here and L.A. I didn't want to wake you, but she's willing to do *A Matter of Honour*.'

'Oh!' Astonished, she took a moment to absorb the news. Mixed feelings coloured her response. 'That's great!' she said finally. Of course it was. 'But can she?'

'She's trying to make the time between other commitments. Will a window of five weeks give you time to shoot her scenes?'

'It'll be tight,' Shannon said, already sorting how it could be done. 'We'll make it possible…somehow,' she decided. 'If necessary, and if she agrees, we could go to shooting six days some weeks without incurring penal rates, and I'm sure the crew won't mind a few long weeks if it means working with Rose Grady. But did she mention money?'

'She said she'd do it for what we can afford. She really liked the script.'

'Oh, that's…that's generous.' Pushing aside all

other considerations, she said, 'Devin, I really do appreciate this. Thank you!'

Reaching out a long arm, he took her hand and drew her closer. 'Thank me properly then?' he suggested, taking her other hand and holding them both in a firm clasp.

Her lips parted slightly as she stared up at him, tempted but reluctant. The memory of her dream surfaced—a dream in which they had been making love with all the fierce mutual passion they used to share, their limbs entwined as he penetrated the innermost warmth of her body. A dream rudely interrupted, leaving lingering desire that still tingled in her breasts and made her body heavy and lethargic.

Colour stung her cheeks, and mutely she shook her head. Temptation was a serpent, much too risky to play with.

'One kiss,' Devin coaxed, his voice deep and lazy, making her toes curl in response, a slow heat rise in her body. 'That's all, I swear. Is it too much to ask?'

He wasn't forcing her, he was asking. There was even a hint of pleading in his voice.

Reluctantly, she moved closer, not quite touching him, and lifted her mouth to his, briefly touched his lips and drew away.

He still held her hands. His eyes were sombre and very dark. He said sternly, 'Don't cheat, Shannon.' Then his hands moved to her waist, bringing her body into contact with his, and his mouth found hers in a devastating erotic exploration.

She put her hands on his arms, intending to resist. The warm, muscled flesh under her fingers was seductive, and her palms lingered, then slid up to his shoulders until she was clinging to him, her eyes closed. He persuaded her mouth to open for him, and her head tipped back as he explored, tasted, giving her a wild, dark pleasure that dreams could only dimly replicate.

Then he lifted his head, and she heard him mutter, 'That's better.'

Rousing a shred of resistance, she opened her eyes and flattened her palms against his chest, and he let her put a few inches of space between them, before his hands reluctantly moved from her waist and she was free.

She had to put a hand on the counter to steady herself, her breath coming in uneven gasps. Tiny waves of heat passed over her, and her legs felt weak. Devin raised a hand to smooth a tendril of hair from her cheek and tuck it behind her ear, and she flinched.

He frowned, dropping his hand. 'I'm not going to touch you again,' he said. 'Would you like some coffee?'

Coffee? For a second the word was meaningless. 'Yes,' she said, then wished she hadn't. But he was drawing up a chair for her and she sank thankfully into it as he poured two cups. At least he wasn't looking at her while she tried to compose herself.

She grabbed the cup he handed her, and scalded her mouth with the first hasty gulp. Devin sat down and drank his in leisurely fashion. His bare chest gleamed under the merciless kitchen lamp. His hair was still untidy and he had a beard shadow on his cheeks. She'd felt the rasp of it when he kissed her.

He looked dangerously sexy.

Shannon wrenched her eyes from him and stared down at her coffee. 'When can Rose come over?' she asked him, forcing her mind to a safe topic.

He didn't answer for a moment or two. Then he said, 'She says in three weeks. If you'd like to phone her back you can discuss it with her.'

'Three weeks!' Her gaze flew to his face.

'Too soon?'

Shannon swallowed. 'It'll be a rush. But we'll do it.'

'Can I help?'

'You?'

He shrugged. 'I've got a stake in this. There must be something I can do. Some donkey work.'

Donkey work? Devin? She couldn't help a small spurt of laughter.

He said curtly, 'I realise I know nothing about film-making—'

'I didn't mean to offend you,' Shannon assured him. 'I'm just surprised at you offering.'

'I'm not a creative person, so I never thought it was much use trying. But there's a lot of peripheral stuff like keeping accounts that I can do.'

It would be a relief to be able to hand over some of the practical responsibility, leaving her free for more creative tasks. 'But do you really have time for this?' she asked. After all, he had his own company to run.

'I'll make time,' he promised.

'Well…thank you. There are some things your business brain would be useful for…'

To accommodate Rose's limited time-frame, there were last-minute changes to the script and the shooting schedules.

The art department redecorated and furnished parts of an old villa in period style, while carpenters were transforming an unused boardroom in a venerable bank building into a nineteenth century courtroom.

The DOP reported problems with the main camera and had to order a part in from Japan, there was a clash with city council regulations regarding parking for the huge vans carrying electrical equipment and props, and catering arrangements needed to be confirmed for the fifty or so people involved on any given day.

Remembering she had a dinner party to organise, Shannon was tempted to call it off, but that would be reneging on her bargain with Devin.

She made it easy by having a catering firm deliver. 'I hope you don't mind,' she said half-defiantly to Devin, 'but I really don't have time to cook, and besides, they'll do it so much better.'

'It seems very sensible,' he told her, 'and I can afford it.'

'I'll pay for it.'

'Don't be silly. I wouldn't have suggested this dinner party if I'd known how tight your shooting schedule would have to be to fit in with Rose.'

With Con and Amy smoothing the wheels, the dinner went better than Shannon expected. She had invited the art director who was working on *A Matter of Honour,* and her husband who managed a boutique art gallery, and the evening went very pleasantly, sometimes even hilariously.

After the guests left Devin closed the door and dropped an arm about Shannon's shoulders as they returned to the living room. 'That went well,' he said. 'I hope you enjoyed yourself too.'

'Did *you?*' She moved away from him when they entered the room, ignoring his slightly crooked smile, his gleaming eyes.

'Very much. Almost like old times.'

It had been, on the surface. He'd smiled at her, teased her gently, sat beside her after dinner with an arm thrown over the sofa back, his thigh warm against hers.

Even when he was deep in conversation with the art director's husband, she'd felt his eyes on her and looked up to meet his lazy smile before he turned back to the other man.

Later while the others talked she'd noticed him sitting silent, his gaze again fixed on her with curious intensity. As soon as her glass was empty he was there with a bottle ready to top it up. And when she left the room to fetch after-dinner mints from the kitchen he came after her to help.

He had been the perfect host, but it was if he had a third eye that was constantly trained on her, making her aware of herself, of her every movement, aware of *him*. And now she was more acutely so than ever, even though they were several feet apart.

Shannon was reminded of other occasions when they'd had guests and could hardly wait until they'd gone before tumbling into each other's arms.

She couldn't help wondering if that was what they would be doing if she'd not enraged him again with her refusal to consider his olive branch while she was filming. Her blood quickened and piercing regret made her breath catch in her chest.

Devin asked if he could come along to watch the first day of filming, and after a moment's hesitation she said of course. 'You'll have to turn off your cell phone while we're shooting,' she warned him.

'I hadn't thought of that,' he confessed. 'I'll tell the office I'll be unavailable.'

'You'll be bored.'

'I'm sure I'll cope.'

Devin had followed her in his own car, and as the crew members arrived and stood about with coffee and toast and muffins, she introduced him as 'My husband, who's financing the film.'

Most of them greeted her with extravagant hugs and kisses, then took Devin's coolly proffered hand and returned his courteous 'Hello' with varying degrees of surprise and grateful enthusiasm.

Craig gave him a casual 'Hi,' and Devin reciprocated with a nod.

Shannon checked the set while sipping coffee from a paper cup. The room had been furnished as a Victorian drawing room with buttoned velvet chairs, polished tables and ornately framed paintings. The camera, sound and lighting crew soon filled the remaining space, lifting equipment from large metal carry boxes and trailing heavy electrical cables across the floor and through the doorway.

Devin leaned against the door jamb, surveying the scene with detached interest. Holding a clipboard, Shannon advised him, 'Don't stand in doorways on a film set.'

He moved into the room as two crew members wearing cargo pants with bulging pockets humped a metal tripod past him and began setting up a white screen. 'What's that for?'

'Lighting—it's a reflector.' Shannon was looking about for the art director. 'Is Sandy here yet?' she asked the room at large.

One of the sound crew looked up from fixing a shaggy wool-covered mike to a long, unwieldy boom. 'Talking to wardrobe, I think.'

Devin had moved into a corner, standing with arms folded.

Shannon finished her coffee and looked about for

somewhere to dump the cup, and he came forward. 'I'll get rid of it for you.'

'Thanks. There'll be a bin about,' she said, going off to confer with the art director.

When she returned Devin was holding a tripod upright while the gaffer placed small sandbags about its base to keep it steady under the heavy lights that it supported.

He made himself unobtrusively useful until everything was in place and Shannon called for a rehearsal.

The actors blocked through their moves for the camera, while Shannon and the director of photography watched on a monitor. The DOP suggested Craig should enter the shot from a different direction, and the art director shifted a table that was impeding the action. They ran through the scene several times before Shannon judged it ready to shoot.

The first take was aborted when a helicopter passed overhead, and the next because the rustle of an actress's taffeta skirts was picked up by the mike as a loud background noise, so she was asked to limit her movements.

By lunchtime they had shot the brief scene four times, and another in the same location.

Devin appeared at Shannon's side as she helped herself to salad and pasta in the room set aside for meals. It echoed with chatter, the bare boards, trestle tables and plastic stackable chairs not absorbing sound.

'Is that all you're having?' he asked.

'Too much to eat makes me sleepy and I need to be on my toes this afternoon.'

He scowled briefly but all he said was, 'Are you happy with this morning's work?'

'We've made a good start. The crew are settling in nicely.' She carried her plate to one of the tables, and he took the empty chair next to hers.

'It's taken a long time to get two short sequences.'

'We're doing okay.'

The director of photography sat down at Devin's other side and soon the two men were deep in a discussion of the mechanics of camera work. Later she saw the DOP demonstrating to Devin how the heavy cameras were raised, lowered, and slid back and forth for different angles. Somewhat to her surprise, Devin was still on the set when the crew packed up for the day. He said to Shannon, 'I'll just drop in at the office on the way, and see you at home, okay?'

'Fine.'

'You won't be hanging about here alone?' he asked.

Shannon shook her head. 'I'll be off soon. Will you be long? I could buy something to eat on my way back to the apartment.'

'About an hour, maybe. Don't wait for me.'

But she did, keeping the tray of Chinese food warm until he arrived.

As they sat down to eat it, he said, 'There's a lot of waiting about on a film set.'

'I told you you'd be bored.'

'I wasn't, but I'm beginning to see why the business

is so expensive, there are so many people and so much equipment involved. And a lot of hanging about waiting. But isn't it difficult for the actors when the script isn't shot in sequence?'

'We try to get all the scenes in one place done before we move to another set.'

'So you don't have to keep moving all the equipment.'

'It saves a lot of time and wear and tear.'

'And when Rose arrives...?' he said.

'Hers should be the only scenes still to be done at the house. Then we shift all the gear to the old bank and film her courtroom scenes first.'

'Makes sense.' He nodded.

'I'm glad you came,' she said impulsively.

'Tomorrow I have a meeting I need to attend, but I'd like to come back another time if I won't be in the way.'

'Fine.' She speared a piece of sweet-and-sour pork. 'I hope...' Shannon toyed with another piece of pork.

'What?'

'Well, you might begin to appreciate the way I feel about filming.' Although it was a bit late for that, she acknowledged sadly.

'I admit I never understood your...absorption in your craft.'

'Aren't you absorbed in what you do?' she queried. 'You're very successful.'

Devin shook his head. 'Printing machines? I could as easily have gone into manufacturing toilet fittings.

Printing was something I happened to know about, but I didn't want to set up a rival company to the family. So I figured there was a future in digital presses if I could find the right people to design and build them. All I wanted was to be independent of the family money, to make my own way.'

'You felt pretty strongly about that.' She knew he'd had to fight considerable opposition from his father.

'More strongly than I've felt about anything—except you.'

Well, at least his business had borne sweeter fruit than his marriage. 'I felt strongly about you too,' she confessed. 'I wanted our marriage to work, Devin.'

'But not enough,' he said, his carefully neutral voice belying the condemnation in the words, 'to stay and *make* it work.'

CHAPTER EIGHT

'IT wasn't all my fault!' Shannon flashed.

'I know that. I've never pretended to be perfect. But when I take on something I don't run out on it when things get tough.'

'No, you just find someone to blame!'

There was a tense silence. 'If I made you feel I was blaming you,' Devin said, 'I apologise. Sincerely. I made mistakes, lost patience when I should have been making an effort to see your point of view, pushed when I should have coaxed. A hundred things I should have done differently.'

'You still think I'm responsible for the miscarriage.'

He threw out an exasperated hand. 'I know you didn't intentionally lose the baby.'

'But you were angry that I did.'

'Yes,' he conceded. Frowning down at his coffee, he said with an apparent effort, 'I was furious with fate for dealing you such a cruel blow. And with myself for not being able to protect you from it…from yourself. Somehow it spilled over into anger at you too, because—' he paused, then went on in a lowered tone '—for a little while I was scared I'd lose you as well the baby.'

'I wasn't in any danger.'

She had always been healthy and strong, and on the farm she'd been accustomed to getting up early and engaging in harder physical work than filming. Laughing off his concerns, Shannon had insisted there was no reason to change her lifestyle for something as natural as pregnancy. 'I'll be one of those women who gives birth in the field and goes back to work with her baby on her back an hour later,' she'd boasted.

Well, she'd been wrong. Apparently she was one of those women who couldn't even carry a baby to term. Four months into the pregnancy it had spontaneously aborted.

Devin's mother had sighed, 'You really shouldn't have kept on working, you know, dear. It's all very well thinking you can manage a career and family, but you need to take care when you're pregnant.'

And Shannon, racked with grief and guilt, was sure Devin tacitly agreed. As she became even further immersed in work, burying the painful memory by exhausting herself into nightly oblivion, Devin had become more and more tight-lipped and uncommunicative, until one evening he'd exploded into unexpected rage, confirming her conviction. 'You put that damned film before me, before our marriage, before your baby,' he had accused her. 'And I'm not prepared to tolerate it any longer.'

'I'm not going to give up my work!' she'd protested, in the grip of a nameless, black terror. 'It's important!' It was a necessary part of her life, her very self.

He'd chosen to misinterpret that. 'Telling pretty stories is vital to the welfare of the world?' he sneered.

'They're not just pretty stories!' Shannon defended herself. 'Films can influence and inform as well as entertain. Do you think what I do is less valuable than making printing presses?'

'That's not the point.'

'I thought it *was* the point you were trying to make. And you work overtime sometimes yourself.'

'*I'm* not carrying a baby! Nor ever likely to be.'

'And because I was you think I should have given up my career?'

'I think you could learn to think of something else besides your precious damned career. You'd never have time for any children we might have, any more than you've time for me, for our marriage.'

She'd tried to assure him that when filming was over she would have more time. 'And the doctors said there's no reason we can't have another baby,' she reminded him. There had been no discernible medical reason for the miscarriage.

'I'm not prepared to risk another pregnancy,' Devin stated flatly, 'unless you stop working.'

But of course she wouldn't. After going on location against Devin's opposition she never returned to their home. Instead she found herself a flat, collected her things from the house and told him it was over.

The first few months had been the hardest, but she'd stuck it out and become almost used to feeling as though she'd cut off a limb—a limb that still reminded her with phantom pain that it had once existed, had once seemed something she could never live without.

Well, she could live without Devin—adequately if not exactly happily.

She had learned to laugh again, to enjoy life, although not with the same singing intensity that had coloured her days since she met him, and to work without guilt nagging at the back of her mind.

Could he really have changed so much, not only tolerating her absorption in work but positively encouraging her? And even offering his own expertise in organisation and finance.

Shannon waited for Devin to complain about the erratic hours she worked, the skipped meals and late nights. Instead he brought coffee to her workroom when she was rearranging her storyboards and shooting schedules after midnight, and encouraged her to discuss the myriad problems that arose in the course of her day.

One night when she was actually home in time for dinner he cooked it, and later poured her coffee and made her sit down and listen to a CD with him. He didn't talk, and after a while she slid into sleep. She was barely conscious of him removing the glass from her hand and then he lifted her into his arms.

Half waking, she murmured a protest that he ignored, and she was sleepily aware of being carried along the passageway and lowered carefully to the bed. He slipped her shoes off, loosened the fastening of her trousers and tucked her under the blankets, making her feel cosseted and deliciously comforted. She felt the warm touch of his lips on her forehead before he turned off the light, and she curled into a foetal position and instantly dropped back into a deep, satisfying sleep.

'I booked Rose in at the Hilton,' she told Devin next morning over a hasty coffee before leaving. 'I guess it's up to her standard.'

'You didn't think of inviting her here?'

'To stay? We don't have room.'

'We would if you moved back in with me.'

'Do you really think your ex-lover would want to stay with us?'

'My what?'

Shannon stirred sugar into her cup. 'You told me you and she had "a thing going" when you were at university. And you've been seeing her regularly for the last couple of years.'

Devin said patiently, 'That "thing" at university was years ago and didn't come to anything. Occasionally we spend a few hours together, catching up and talking over old times. She's homesick and sometimes likes to be with a fellow Kiwi.'

'I still don't imagine she'd want to stay here.' Compromising, Shannon suggested, 'If she's not too jet-lagged, she might like to have dinner with us after she arrives.'

'That would be a nice gesture,' Devin agreed.

'She won't want a limo when she flies in, will she?' Someone would have to pick her up.

'I told her I'd collect her.'

Shannon looked up. 'You're not too busy?'

'I thought it would help you out.'

'I'm sure she'd appreciate that, if you'd like to do it.'

Several times Devin dropped in for a couple of hours and watched the filming. The cast and crew began to take his presence for granted, and were happy to regale him with the technical details of their jobs.

The day Rose was due to arrive shooting was up to schedule, and when they had completed the last footage for the day Shannon thought it might save time if they blocked out the next morning's scene involving Rose and Craig. Besides, she was a little nervous of working with an established star and wanted Rose to have confidence in her as a director.

Shannon's first assistant stood in for Rose, going through the scene, but it didn't seem to be working. Eventually Shannon went over to show her what she wanted.

Rose's character was upset and angry, pacing about the room while arguing with her fiancé, until he took her in his arms and kissed her. Their positions relative to the camera were crucial, so that just before the kiss their expressions would be caught on film.

Standing with Craig's arm about her waist and her hands on his shoulders, Shannon curved her back and turned her head slightly.

'That's it,' the DOP said, his eyes fixed on the monitor. 'Craig, just move your head a bit to the left.

That's what we want. Brilliant.' Craig, his face inches from hers, grinned down at Shannon. 'Got it,' he said, and bent her further over his arm in a dramatic move that unbalanced her and she had to clutch at him, as he dropped a cheeky kiss on her mouth.

He hauled her upright amid a few teasing whoops and whistles, and she looked over his shoulder and saw Devin, an arctic expression on his face, in the doorway.

Craig released her, and as Devin moved forward into the room she realised he wasn't alone. There was no mistaking Rose Grady's almost ethereal beauty, made more so by faint shadows beneath her large, hauntingly blue eyes after her long trip.

She barely reached Devin's shoulder, which was close behind her. He had a protective hand on her waist.

Some actresses in real life were ordinary, almost plain, only blooming under the camera lens which by some strange symbiosis loved them. Rose didn't need the camera to prove she was as delicately seductive as her name.

Shannon hurried across the floor. 'Rose! Hello, I'm Shannon Cleary. I didn't expect you on set today.'

'She insisted,' Devin explained as Rose took Shannon's outstretched hand and gave her the smile that had melted a million male hearts. 'We haven't even been to her hotel yet.'

'I wanted to meet you and see the set,' Rose told

Shannon. 'It will help me get straight into the character tomorrow.'

'I was just standing in for you,' Shannon said.

Craig sauntered up behind her. She introduced them and watched him fall under the woman's spell. Other crew members crowded around and Rose charmed them all, saying how much she looked forward to working again in her homeland.

Then Devin bent his head close to her and said, 'I'll take you to your hotel, and later Shannon and I would like you to join us for dinner if you're up to it.'

'Oh, that's nice of you,' Rose answered, 'but I need an early night. Why don't you have dinner with me at the hotel? We could talk a little,' she added to Shannon. 'Maybe Craig too?' She smiled at him again. 'I should get to know my leading man.'

'You don't have to do that,' Shannon assured her, 'if you'd rather just eat alone and go to bed.'

'Oh, no! Please come, all of you. I'll look forward to it.'

'All right, thank you.' Shannon wasn't dressed for dinner at the Hilton; she'd have to go home and change first. 'We'll be along later.'

'Meet you in the bar, then,' Rose said gaily. 'About seven?'

Devin didn't come back to change, and Shannon showered quickly, washed and dried her hair, put on a silky bronze shift, a transparent, floaty gold wrap, and some makeup, and took a taxi to the hotel.

When she walked into the bar Rose and Devin were seated side by side on a deeply upholstered leather banquette drinking sparkling wine from glass flutes. Rose had her head tilted to one side, listening avidly to Devin. She was wearing a pale pink dress with a short skirt that showed off her wonderful legs. Her narrow, elegant feet were clad in matching pink sandals. Even if her face hadn't been so well-known she would have drawn every eye in the crowded bar.

Devin turned his head and broke off what he was saying, rising as Shannon approached. He reached out a hand and drew her to him, brushing a kiss across her cheek. 'Hello, darling. What can I get you to drink?'

She asked for gin and tonic and sat down in one of the two chairs facing the banquette. 'I didn't ask how your trip was,' she said to Rose, summoning a smile.

'Oh, long and tiring, but Devin's looked after me wonderfully since I landed.' She followed his progress across the room with her eyes. 'You're a lucky woman.'

Shannon had no idea what to say to that. How much did Rose know about Devin's marriage and the breakup? She smiled again, stiffly. 'So are you, although I know talent has as much to do with your success as luck.'

Rose gave a little laugh. 'I did have good luck, being in the right place at the right time, but I worked hard to get to that place.'

'I know.' Had she sounded bitchy? Shannon hoped not. 'You're a brilliant actress. And I'm really grateful that you agreed to be in *A Matter of Honour*.'

'I loved the script,' Rose said eagerly. 'And Devin is very persuasive.'

'He can be…persuasive,' Shannon agreed.

'Besides,' Rose flashed her bewitching smile, 'he made me an offer I couldn't refuse. Oh, here comes Craig.' She waved and beckoned him over.

A waiter came by and Craig ordered himself a beer, then sat by Rose. Returning with drinks, Devin had no choice but to take the seat beside Shannon, and when they went into dinner they ended up in the same formation at the table.

Rose wanted to know how far they'd got with the filming, and was keen to discuss her part. Devin said little, and by the time they were having coffee he was leaning back, his chair pushed slightly away from the table as he watched and listened.

When Rose had to stifle a yawn he said, 'We'd better leave you to get some sleep.'

As they made a move to leave Rose said, 'What time do you want me, Shannon?'

'Is eight too early? I'll send someone to pick you up.'

'I'll do that,' Devin said swiftly.

Rose leaned over to touch his arm. 'Thank you, Dev.' She turned to Shannon. 'Eight o'clock, then.'

In the morning Rose turned up looking like the flower she'd been named for, fresh and dewy and beautiful. Even more so after wardrobe and makeup had transformed her into a demure Victorian maiden. But there was a hold-up when she found she was tripping over her gown, and returned to wardrobe to have the problem fixed.

Everyone relaxed while they waited, reading newspapers, chatting, and drinking coffee. Devin strolled over to where Shannon was poring over the scene list on her clipboard.

'Did you have breakfast?' he asked her.

'I had coffee.'

'I'll get you something to eat.'

Before she could protest he'd gone, to return minutes later with a couple of buttered muffins on a plate.

'You need a minder,' he said.

'I'm fine.' She took one of the muffins and bit into it. 'But thanks.'

Craig came over to ask her, 'Are we going with the way we blocked the scene last night?'

'Yes,' she told him. 'We'll have to take Rose through it.'

'Fine by me.' Craig grinned. 'I reckon it'll take a few rehearsals of that kiss.'

'Rose is very professional,' she reminded him cruelly, hiding a smile. 'She'll probably get it right first time.'

Craig shook his head sorrowfully. 'Oh, dang. I was looking forward to this.'

'You still get to kiss Rose Grady.'

'Yeah, so I do.' He brightened. 'And here she is again.' Rose had appeared in the doorway, and he went to lead her on to the set.

Devin murmured, 'Your friend Craig seems rather smitten with Rose.'

Shannon answered distractedly, signalling to her assistant director to call the cast to their places. 'Aren't all the men? He's supposed to be in love with her, after all.'

She watched the two principals take their positions. The first assistant called for silence. The DOP joined Shannon at the monitor, and Devin retreated to lean against a wall.

From the moment they started to rehearse, the chemistry between Rose and Craig was palpable, much to Shannon's relief. Sometimes actors had to work hard at feigning attraction but this wasn't going to be a problem, and their instant rapport would add authenticity and tension to their screen relationship.

When the assistant director called 'Cut!' after the first take of the kiss Craig reluctantly released Rose and drawled, 'Aw, spoilsport.'

The crew laughed, and Rose joined in. The assistant director looked at Shannon and she said, 'We'll have one more take.'

Craig winked at her. 'Thanks, doll.'

Next time she looked up Devin had disappeared. She wasn't sure when he had left, but supposed he'd gone to his office.

CHAPTER NINE

THE day's shooting encountered few hitches, and when she sent off the rolls of film for processing Shannon was satisfied with progress.

Devin appeared again to drive Rose back to her hotel, but it was several hours before Shannon joined him at the apartment after viewing the previous day's rushes.

He poured her a drink that she gratefully accepted. 'Thanks for looking after Rose,' she said.

'Not a problem.' He seemed restless, handing her drink to her, prowling to the window, taking a cursory glance at the view, then getting himself a whisky and hesitating before coming back to sit opposite her. 'How is she doing?' he asked at last.

Shannon licked the liqueur from her lips. 'Great. I can't thank you enough.' Remembering, she added, looking at him questioningly, 'She said you made an offer she couldn't refuse.'

'I told you she wanted to come home for a while.'

'That's not all though, is it? What did you offer her?'

'That's confidential. Between her and me.'

'You're paying her over budget, aren't you?'

'I'm protecting my investment.'

She saw she would get no more from him. 'Well…thank you again. She'll certainly add something special to the film.'

'And that's all that matters to you, isn't it? Personal considerations don't come into it.'

Cautiously, she queried, 'What personal considerations?'

'For instance,' he said, 'jealousy.'

Shannon flushed; she couldn't help it. Of course she was jealous, had been ever since Devin mentioned his relationship with Rose Grady. No matter that he'd said any romantic involvement was all in the past, had scarcely even existed. No matter that her feelings were irrational.

He'd said Shannon would be the only woman in his life as long as she stayed with him. And she believed he meant it when he said he wanted to give their marriage a chance. Devin had always been a man of his word.

But that was before she'd seen Rose in the flesh. The star's breathtaking beauty, the ethereal glow that seemed to surround her, was enough to make any other woman feel insecure, even if she was certain of her man. And Shannon wasn't.

How could a normal male help falling at least a little under the spell of such an exquisite creature? If he'd been attracted to her in his university days, surely he must find her stunning now. She even had a personality that matched her face.

Devin stood up, so suddenly that Shannon started.

He stayed looking down at her, then tossed off his drink and went to get another. 'So you're not entirely immune,' he said.

Watching his back warily, she said, 'Immune?'

Turning, he lifted his glass and drank again. 'It shows you're human after all.'

'You know I'm human! And so are you,' she added involuntarily. Under his usually controlled exterior, Shannon knew Devin was a very sensual man, not cut out for the celibacy she'd forced on him.

'Yes, I am,' he agreed calmly, but his eyes held a warning glitter. 'So don't push me too far, Shannon.'

A tremor of fear laced with jealousy ran through her, and she felt her body tense. But her mind shied away. She didn't want to think about this. 'I'm tired. It's been a busy day.'

'Scared?' he jeered as she bent and put her glass on a side table.

'Should I be?' She looked straight at him, her head tilted defiantly.

He gave a harsh bark of a laugh. 'Maybe. I never thought I'd be tempted to use force on a woman.'

Her eyes widened momentarily, her heart giving a thud of fear before it steadied. She knew him well enough to be ninety-nine percent certain he would never carry out the implied threat. Even admitting the temptation was a breach of his rigid code of conduct.

The one percent of doubt must have shown in her face.

'Oh, don't worry,' he said. 'I still have some self-control left, I hope—as I proved last time I came close to letting my baser nature get the better of me. But this situation can't last.'

He must feel caught between a rock and a hard place—his wife refused to sleep with him, yet he'd sworn himself to a barren fidelity. And now there was Rose, with her air of innocent sensuality. Shannon recalled how he'd quietly, abruptly disappeared while they were filming the kiss.

She should tell him she wouldn't hold him to his word, only she couldn't bring herself to do it. Guiltily she knew she was being unfair, a bitch in the manger, but the thought of him making love to someone else was physically painful, squeezing at her heart. 'You set out the conditions,' she reminded him.

'I made my bed and now I can lie on it?' He laughed again, without humour. 'It's exactly what I'd like to do, but not alone.'

Shannon wanted to defuse the prickly atmosphere, tempted to give in and offer to share his bed after all, but his mood wasn't loving or conciliatory. It didn't seem the right moment. 'I'll see you in the morning,' she said, turning toward the passageway and proceeding to her bedroom without looking back.

Rose was easy to work with and generous with her co-star. She never tried to steal scenes from him or anyone else, and wasn't temperamental. It was impossible to dislike her.

She agreed to come to dinner at the weekend and

when Shannon told Devin she'd asked Craig along he raised his brows but said nothing. The two of them arrived together on Saturday evening and put on what Shannon could only think of as a performance.

Sparking off each other, they were charming and funny and entertaining.

Devin was an urbane host, keeping the wine flowing as Shannon served the meal, and content to let their guests do most of the talking. Shannon noticed him regarding Rose with a smile curving his mouth, and warmth in his eyes, while she acted out an amusing on-set incident from her Hollywood experience, using her graceful hands expressively, her sapphire-blue eyes alight with laughter.

Devin laughed too, at the end of the story, and Shannon forced herself to join in. Her hands were curled in her lap, the nails digging into her palms. It was a long time since she had heard Devin truly laugh, she realised bleakly. Laughter had once been a part of their life together. Now it was rare, and too often laced with bitterness.

Looking away, Shannon found Craig's curious gaze on her face, and gave him a forced smile. She stood up and began clattering dishes together. 'I'll get the dessert,' she said brightly. 'Back in a couple of minutes.'

In the kitchen she rinsed the dishes and stacked them quickly in the dishwasher, closed it and stood for a moment clutching the edge of the counter, her head bowed. Then jumped as Craig's voice said, 'Are you okay?'

Turning, she pinned a smile into place. 'Fine,' she lied.

He had two serving dishes of leftovers in his hands. 'Where do you want these?'

'In the fridge if there's room.' She opened it and took out mousse and cheesecake, putting them on the counter.

'You sure?' Craig queried.

'There's space now.' She picked up a cake slice to cut the desserts into segments for serving.

He placed the dishes on the shelves and closed the door. 'I mean, are you sure you're okay? Come on,' he coaxed, 'tell Uncle Craig all about it.'

Touched, she shook her head. He might seem all froth and bubble on the surface, but underneath Craig had a sensitive, intuitive streak that made him a good actor, able to empathise with other people's feelings. 'Nothing to tell,' she said. 'I'm a bit tired, maybe.'

He and Rose must be tired too, but it didn't seem to be affecting their spirits. She cut the last slice and brushed a strand of hair from her eyes.

Craig was regarding her with his head cocked to one side. 'Okay, don't tell me. But have a hug anyway.'

His arms came round her and with a small laugh she relaxed against him. It was a comforting, sexless embrace and just what she needed. Some of the tension drained out of her and she rested her head against his shoulder before drawing away. 'You're so nice, Craig. Thanks.'

'Any time.'

He smiled at her, his eyes concerned, and she turned to put down the cake slice and pick up the desserts. 'Can you bring in that stack of bowls?'

'Sure.' He followed her back to the dining room. Devin had shifted his chair, angling it closer to Rose's, and she was leaning forward, her exquisite face lifted to his as she spoke in a low tone.

They looked up as the other two entered, and Rose gave a small gurgle of laughter. 'You've started on the dessert already?' she asked Craig. When he looked blank, she pointed out, 'You have cream and chocolate on your sleeve.'

'I'm sorry!' Shannon took a napkin and wiped it off. 'It must have come from the cake slice when...' When he hugged her. She stopped, embarrassed.

Craig grinned, taking his place again. 'No harm done.'

Shannon couldn't help smiling back. Then she saw Devin's cool, narrowed gaze shift from Craig to her, and the smile died on her lips.

Devin picked up the half-empty wine bottle and filled Rose's glass, then hesitated as he poised the bottle over Craig's. 'You're not driving Rose back to her hotel, are you?'

'We'll be taking a taxi.'

Devin nodded and topped up the glass.

He looked strangely grim, though he remained the

perfect host until he closed the door behind the guests and followed Shannon back to the dining room where she began clearing the remains.

Devin gathered a couple of wineglasses and an empty bottle into his hands. 'They've gone off in the same cab,' he said. 'What's the odds they're going to be sharing a bed as well?'

Shannon shrugged, taking a stack of cups and saucers into the kitchen. If Craig took Rose from Devin's orbit she couldn't be sorry.

'It doesn't bother you?' He placed the glasses and bottle on the counter, and when she turned from putting the cups and saucers in the dishwasher he was disconcertingly close.

'All I'm concerned about is that they do a good job on the film,' she said.

His eyelids flickered, and she thought she'd hit a raw spot.

It was unlike him to speculate on other people's sex lives, but maybe he had a vested interest in Rose's.

Feeling a reluctant compunction, she said, 'If they're having an affair it will probably only last as long as they're filming. Sometimes actors get caught up in their roles and confuse them with reality for a while.'

'Very pragmatic,' he said. 'So tell me how Craig managed to get dessert on his sleeve?'

The change of topic disconcerted her. For a second she contemplated concocting some plausible scenario, but why lie to him? She had nothing to be ashamed of. 'He gave me a hug,' she said, 'while I was cutting up the mousse.'

Devin stilled a quick movement. 'A hug?'

'He thought I needed some…comfort.' Catching a quick, disbelieving curl of his lip, she said sharply, 'We weren't indulging in a passionate embrace!'

'Why did you need a hug?'

When she didn't answer, he said, 'If you wanted comforting you could have come to me.'

'You?' She was startled.

His mouth tightened. 'Your husband. Is that idea so repugnant?'

'You didn't offer it,' she said, bemused. 'And besides…' Besides, he was the cause of her unhappiness.

'You never wanted it from me, did you?' he said, unexpectedly caustic. 'Not even after the baby.'

'Why do you say that?'

'You pushed me away.'

The first few days were still a blur in her memory. She vaguely recalled being given pills, taking them without question, hoping they would help to dull the pain. 'No,' she said. 'I wouldn't have…'

'When I held you,' Devin said, 'you went rigid, as though you could barely tolerate it.'

That was quite likely true. 'I was afraid,' she said numbly. 'I felt as though I'd break apart if I accepted sympathy.'

He stared at her. In an almost hostile tone, he asked, 'And is that why as soon as you were out of hospital you insisted on going to work? I hardly saw you for days at a time.'

'I needed something to stop me thinking about the baby. It hurt so much, and working was the only thing that could make me forget,' she said. 'At least sometimes. And I suppose…it made me feel less of a failure.'

'A *failure?*'

'As a woman, a mother. A wife. Filming was the one thing I knew I was good at.'

That seemed to have shaken him. 'Having a miscarriage didn't make you a failure as woman!'

'I felt I'd let you down, let our baby down. And you…you thought so.'

'Shannon—no!'

'You practically said it. Your mother too.'

'I said a number of things in the heat of anger that I didn't really mean, and that I've regretted ever since.' He briefly massaged the back of his neck, scowling. 'I felt inadequate too, and guilty because I hadn't made you take things easier, hadn't saved you from the pain you were going through. Afterwards, you didn't seem to need me or even want me, and I knew I'd failed you but I didn't know what to do about it.'

'You didn't fail me,' she said. 'I simply had to cope in the only way I knew.'

Devin shook his head. 'What do you mean?'

She had to think about that before she could explain. 'I did what my father had done after my mother died,' she said hesitantly. 'He said crying didn't do any good, it wouldn't bring her back, and we had to get on with life.'

Devin was staring at her. 'You were twelve years old!'

Shannon nodded. 'Dad worked out his grief with physical labour—he re-fenced the whole farm in the months after she died, built a new hayshed…anything to keep him from thinking, I guess. Fixing things.' To make up for not being able to fix the illness that had killed his wife, she supposed. 'Tears made him feel helpless, and he hated that.'

'And so, when he died…?'

'It was…awful. I couldn't help thinking that if I'd looked for him sooner…if I'd been with him…if I'd helped more he might not have been so tired that he was careless…all the what-ifs…' She was looking down at her hands, fingers twisting.

Devin reached out and took them in his strong, warm clasp. 'I know how that feels. It was like that for me after you left. Did you cry for him?'

She looked up. 'I cried all the way back to the house, running over the paddocks, it seemed for miles, to get to the phone. I was so scared. I called for an ambulance but I knew it was too late. Then I phoned a neighbour to come with his tractor…Dad was pinned, you see, and I couldn't get him out on my own. It was a nightmare. But afterwards there was so much to do…the funeral, keeping the farm going until it was sold—although the neighbours were great—and then there were lawyers and estate agents to deal with. And the inquest. There was no time to cry, and when it was all over it seemed too late. I was numb, but then I moved to Auckland, got involved in my film course and pushed it all to the back of my mind, went on with my life…like he would have wanted.'

'You never told me all this.'

When he had asked about her parents she'd told him the bare facts, and he had respected her obvious reluctance to discuss their deaths. 'I've never told anyone.'

'I wish I'd known.'

She made to move her hands out of his hold, but instead of releasing her he pulled her closer and put his arms about her.

Her cheek was against his shirt and she could smell the scent of his skin. Her hands were flattened on his chest, the beat of his heart against her palm.

It was a tender embrace, rare and infinitely precious. Overwhelming longing stole over her, laced with sadness. It was years since they had been this close emotionally. And maybe it was too late.

There was no passion now in his touch. Like Craig, he'd seen she needed comfort and he was willing to give her that.

A kindness.

Kindness wasn't what she wanted from him.

She stirred against the tempting warmth of his body, then forced herself to move back. His arms tightened momentarily before they fell away.

Shannon ducked her head, smoothing a strand of hair back behind her ear. Fleetingly she glanced at him. His face was grave and intent.

She recalled him saying he had loved her. But had she killed that love with her desertion, her suspicion of his motives, her refusal to accept his physical passion?

'Shannon,' he said, 'we need to talk…'

She was a coward, afraid of what he might say…perhaps that his experiment had failed because of her lack of co-operation, and he didn't want her anymore. Maybe the suspicion that Craig was with Rose tormented him, and he might lose her if he was still tied to Shannon.

The phone shrilled, making her jump. It was late for anyone to be making a call.

Devin let it ring four times, then swore softly and strode across the room to pick up the receiver.

The conversation was short, but when he put the receiver down he turned to Shannon and said, 'Bad news. My father's been taken to hospital with a suspected heart attack.'

CHAPTER TEN

'OH, DEVIN!' Shannon went toward him, but he was already on his way out of the room.

'My mother's distraught,' he said, hurrying to the bedroom. 'I'd better get over there right away.' He scooped his wallet and car keys from the dressing table and grabbed a jacket from the wardrobe.

'I'll come with you.'

She raced into her room, collected her purse and shoes, and joined Devin in the passageway.

Getting to the hospital seemed to take an age. Ralph was in the intensive care unit, and they found Marcia and Lila in the waiting room, both pale and for once less than perfectly groomed.

'Devin! Thank God.' Marcia flung herself into his arms.

His own face haggard, he looked at Lila over his mother's head. 'What's happening?'

'They're working on him.' Lila was standing too. 'We were allowed in for a little while but they have to do some tests, they said. He looks…awful.' Her voice sank to a whisper.

Shannon moved over to Lila and put an arm about her. 'I'm so sorry,' she said.

Marcia lifted her head and wiped a tear with her

160

fingers. 'Shannon.' She seemed to notice her for the first time. 'It's good of you to come.' She turned back to Devin. 'They won't tell us anything.'

Lila said, 'They're still trying to stabilise him.'

'But it's been so long!' Marcia's voice rose. 'And we don't know what's happening!'

'Why don't you sit down,' Devin suggested, his hand urging her to do so, 'and maybe Shannon could bring you and Lila some coffee.'

'Yes,' Shannon agreed instantly. 'And something to eat?'

'I don't want to eat!' Marcia wailed.

Devin said, 'You need to keep your strength up to help Dad through this.'

By the time Shannon returned with sandwiches and coffee, Lila was alone in the waiting room. 'We're allowed in, two at a time,' she said. 'Thanks, Shannon.' She took the polystyrene cup Shannon handed her.

'How are you feeling?'

'I'm okay.' Lila removed the lid and sipped at the coffee, then grimaced. 'Well, I'm holding up. How's Devin?'

It came as a small shock that Lila assumed she'd know how Devin was, under his determined control. 'I'm not sure,' Shannon admitted. 'Where's Payton?' There had been no sign of Lila's husband.

'Payton? He's away. He's been away a lot lately. Business trips, or so he says.' Her mouth curved downward. 'I left a message on his mobile phone.'

Normally, Shannon was sure, Lila would have allowed her teeth to be pulled one by one before confiding her marital troubles to her sister-in-law. But the circumstances were not normal, and maybe she gained some relief from worrying about her father by talking about something—anything—else.

'Are you sure they're not genuine business trips?' she asked tentatively. 'Payton seems devoted to you.'

'Devoted? Does he?' Lila appeared to consider that. 'We've never had fireworks in our relationship, you know. None of that scorching heat that you and Devin generated when you were first married.'

Shannon flushed. Had their mutual passion shown? She'd thought Devin, at least, hid his feelings well, but Lila had known him all her life.

Lila went on, 'I used to congratulate myself after you broke up, that we weren't like that.' She cast a sideways glance at Shannon. 'I suppose because I'd been a bit jealous. I was able to say, "See, it doesn't last." Payton was my best friend. I thought we understood each other, and our marriage was rock-solid, even if it wasn't exciting. Well, I'm not so smug anymore. Maybe exciting was what he really wanted.'

Shannon gave a cracked little laugh. 'And I envied you,' she confessed. 'You and Payton were so well suited, not like Devin and me.'

Lila looked surprised. 'But you're so alike!'

'Alike?'

'Both determined, independent, successful at what

'you do. You don't look to other people for validation, and you hate to admit any weakness.'

Shannon had worked hard at being self-sufficient, emulating her father's stoicism. And, she realised, she'd married a man like him, a staunch, strong-willed man, reluctant to parade his emotions to the world.

'I knew Devin was suffering after you lost that baby,' Lila told her, 'though he'd have died rather than show it in public. And you went back to work almost as if nothing had happened. It must have cost you.'

'Yes.' It had, ultimately, cost her the man she loved, their life together.

The door opened and Devin emerged. 'Your turn,' he said to Lila. 'Try to get Mum to come and have something to eat, will you?'

'Will do.' Lila stood up and he took her place as she hurried into the ward.

'There's coffee,' Shannon said, handing him a cup. 'How is he?'

He filled her in as far as he could while he drank the coffee. 'They're doing all they can,' he finished. 'We can only hope and pray.'

They did that through the night and all day Sunday, their own problems pushed to the background by the crisis. Shannon ensured that food and hot drinks were available to sustain the family, and did her best to maintain their fragile hopes.

In the afternoon Payton arrived, and when Lila came out of the ward he hurried to her and folded her into his arms, saying, 'My poor, dear girl! I came as soon as I got your message.'

Toward evening Ralph was holding his own, and Marcia was persuaded to allow Lila to drive her home and stay with her.

Devin promised faithfully to sit by his father until their return, and call immediately if there was any change. 'If you want to go,' he told Shannon, 'take the car. I don't know when I'll be home.'

Shannon shook her head. Devin loved his father despite their occasional differences, and if he was keeping vigil she wanted to be with him.

In the eerie dimness of the intensive care unit with its arcane machinery, glowing monitors and soft-footed nurses, Shannon tried to conceal her shock at how ill his father looked.

Devin took her hand. 'He's okay for the moment. And he's in the best place possible.'

'I know.' Her fingers curled about his. She was supposed to be comforting *him.*

They sat side by side in high-backed, hard vinyl chairs. Ralph seemed to be sleeping. Shannon reached out with her free hand and stroked his arm, finding it reassuringly warm. She sat back, letting out a small sigh.

'Thanks for staying, Shannon.' Devin hadn't let go her hand. Lifting it, he pressed his lips to her skin, and as he raised his head she involuntarily touched his face, his lean cheek rough with unshaven bristles against the curve of her palm.

He stilled as if afraid to move, his eyes dark and unfathomable, only inches from hers. 'Why did you?' he asked.

'I thought you might need someone,' she told him, and moved her hand from his cheek to smooth his hair back from his forehead. 'I'm your wife. This is my place.'

Devin made the faintest movement of his head, almost as if he had heard some inaudible sound. 'Shannon,' he breathed. Then he closed the small gap between them and found her mouth with his.

It was a kiss of unprecedented tenderness and muted passion that she returned in kind, her hand resting on his nape, her head tilted, lips parted.

Devin drew back reluctantly, but her hand still nestled in his strong fingers. He closed his eyes briefly and let out a sigh. Then a nurse came to check the machines by the bed, murmuring a few encouraging words.

The dim light, the stillness of the patients, and the steady beeping of the machines were hypnotic. After a while Shannon's lids drooped and she fell into a half doze.

When she stirred, she saw that Devin's head was resting on the back of his chair and his eyes were closed again. But he half opened them as she studied him, and smiled at her. 'Still here?' he said, his voice low and indistinct. 'Don't leave me.'

'I won't, not while you need me.'

He sat up, seemingly shaking himself into wakefulness, and looked at his father. He leaned forward to peer at his watch, and turned to Shannon, eyes now fully open. 'You have to work tomorrow.'

'Don't *you?*'

'I can delegate, and do a lot by phone. It's after midnight. Why don't you go home and get some sleep?'

'You just asked me not to leave.'

'I'd been dreaming. There's no need for you to stay.'

There was a stir in the doorway, and his mother tiptoed in. A whispered conference, then Devin put a compelling hand on Shannon's arm. 'Come on, I'm taking you home.'

At the car she said, 'Would you like me to drive?'

'I'm all right.'

He seemed preoccupied on the way to the apartment, and once there Shannon said, 'Can I get you something?'

Devin shook his head. 'You'd better turn in. You've only a few hours to go before you need to be at work.'

The crew would be there and she couldn't dump her assistant director in it with few clues about Shannon's concept of the scenes. 'Are you going to bed?'

Devin passed a hand over his hair. 'I guess. Lila promised to phone if…I'm needed.'

'Would you…' Shannon hesitated. 'Would you like company?'

He studied her. 'A charity case?' he said.

'I just thought you might want…'

'Sympathy, comfort…sex? Choose one, or all three?' His mouth moved crookedly. 'I appreciate the offer,' he told her, 'but I'll pass, thanks. It's been a long day and I don't need any more complications.'

Swallowing the hurt of rejection, Shannon said, 'Let me know if there's anything I can do.'

When she got up Devin was already gone. She hadn't heard the phone, but perhaps he'd just driven to the hospital anyway. Feeling guilty at having slept, she phoned patient inquiries and was told that Mr Keynes was 'holding his own,' which told her nothing new. She debated trying Devin's cell phone but remembered the hospital discouraged their use.

She made herself coffee and raced off to the location.

This was the last day of filming in the house, and by midafternoon she hoped they'd be moving to the garden for some outdoor scenes. Shannon had a consultation with her assistant director, unable to keep herself from glancing at her watch every few minutes, and after an hour she drove back to the hospital.

Payton was in the waiting room, leafing through a magazine. 'Ralph's improving,' he told Shannon. 'They think he could be out of the ICU in a day or two if it continues. Did you see Devin?'

'I thought he was here.'

'He went to the set to tell you the good news. You must have passed each other on the way. He said you switch off your phone when you're filming, and you'd be working until at least six.'

'The cast and crew will be, I left them to it. How long have you been sitting here?'

He shrugged. 'Hours, but that's okay. Lila needs me.'

'Yes,' Shannon said. 'I think she does.'

Payton flicked her an alert look. 'They don't like to think they can't manage alone, these Keyneses. But at times like this they need their loved ones just like us ordinary mortals.'

'I'm sure Lila's a very ordinary mortal,' Shannon said. 'I mean, a very normal woman, needing love and affection…comfort.'

'I know. I've always tried to give it to her, even when she was pretending she didn't need it.'

'She pretends?'

He nodded. 'But after six years of marriage I can read her like a book.'

'Oh?'

Payton frowned. 'What does that mean?'

'Nothing, except…are you sure?'

'What are you getting at, Shannon?'

'It's none of my business.' She regretted showing her scepticism.

'We're family,' he said. 'Spill it.'

'Lila said you're spending a lot of time away from home. It…worries her.'

'Oh, hell! I thought I was covering it so well.'

'Then you *are* having an affair?'

'*Affair?*' Payton coloured angrily. 'Of course not! Whatever gave you that idea?'

'I'm sorry, it's just that…' She broke off, afraid of making things worse. 'I'm sorry,' she repeated.

'*Lila* thinks that?' Payton thrust a hand over his almost non-existent hair. 'I've been working on a deal with a bigger company. It will mean more income but fewer hours for me. Lila and I would like a family, and this way I'd be able to help more, so she could keep on working. I meant to surprise her.' He rubbed a hand over his eyes. 'How could she think…?'

'You just said,' she reminded him, 'that the Keyneses aren't as secure as they pretend to be.' Even Devin wasn't, she'd discovered.

'But Lila knows I adore her!'

The door from the ward opened and Lila stood there. 'What?' she said, her gaze fixed on her husband.

He crossed the room and took her in his arms, giving her a kiss square on her mouth. 'I love you, Lilly-pilly. You know that.'

Lilly-pilly. Shannon blinked, then picked up a magazine and flipped it open.

'I suppose so,' Lila was saying in a dazed voice.

Payton gave a growl in his throat, and Shannon choked down laughter. He seemed such a mild man, but evidently there was a tiger hidden inside somewhere. 'Later,' he promised, 'I'll prove it to you.'

Lila's whisper was scandalised. 'Payton! Stop it!' Then she said, 'Shannon, we didn't expect you so early.'

When Shannon looked up again they were two feet apart, but Lila's cheeks were rosy and Payton looked faintly smug. 'Why don't you two go and have a coffee or something,' she suggested. 'I can wait with your mother.'

Payton said, 'Thanks, Shannon,' and carried his bewildered wife off with a masterly air.

Devin arrived soon afterward, brushing off Shannon's apology for his wasted journey. 'They told me you were here,' he said. 'You'll want to get back.'

'It's all right, I've left my assistant in charge. I'd like to see your father if they'll let me.'

Ralph was conscious, looking considerably better, and at dinnertime he urged his wife to go and have a meal at a nearby restaurant with the rest of the family.

Relief and a bottle of wine helped to lessen the strain they'd been under, and Shannon, who had seen a side of the reserved Keynes family that had been invisible to her before, was more relaxed than she had ever been in their company.

They took Marcia in to say goodnight to her husband, and Shannon murmured to Devin, 'Could you stay with your mother tonight? Payton's back and Lila might like to be at home with him.'

He gave her a slightly surprised look. 'I guess so, but I wouldn't be surprised if Mum insists she's okay on her own.'

Neither would Shannon, but actually Marcia made only a token objection.

*　　*　　*

The film crew had experienced some problems with the garden scenes. Shortly after they set up the cameras the cloudless sky had altered, and changes in the light ruined several takes. In the end they had to stop shooting early.

'It's just bad luck,' Shannon told her apologetic assistant, though she'd hoped to move on to the courthouse set next day.

In the morning it was raining, and the forecast was for more rain the following day. Shannon had to decide whether to stay at the house and film between showers, or move the cameras and equipment to the next set where they could shoot indoors, but then they'd have to bring everything back later, with all the possible continuity hassles that might create.

She decided to stay put, throwing out the tight shooting schedule rather badly, even after a hasty reshuffling of some outdoor scenes to the interior.

Which meant going to six days a week and working at night to get Rose's scenes finished before her deadline.

Devin was also catching up on his own work, in between visiting his father and looking out for his mother. He didn't turn up on the set again until late one evening as they were shooting Rose's final scenes, when her character was watching her sister and her fiancé take their turns in the witness box.

There was a lot of tension on the set. The scene was a crucial turning point, and Rose had no lines but was required to express a changing range of deep emotion without words and without moving from her seat.

Rose gave a powerful performance, and on the last take Shannon felt a rare tingle up her spine that told her this time they had something quite extraordinary.

The rest of the crew knew it too. When the first assistant called, *Cut* they burst into applause.

Rose gave them a Victorian curtsey in acknowledgement, and looked to Shannon for her approval, but Shannon was already out of her chair and crossing the room to give her a congratulatory hug. 'Thank you!' she said sincerely. 'That was great.'

Behind her, Devin's voice said, with a tinge of awe, 'I could almost believe it was real, in spite of the cameras.'

He bent to kiss Rose's cheek as Shannon moved aside. 'Are you all right?'

Rose smiled up at him. 'A bit wrung out.' She turned back to Shannon. 'Is that it?'

'Yes. You've been wonderful, Rose.'

'I've enjoyed it. Everything's so laid-back here, and I love the way the crew and the actors all help each other out.'

Then someone called, 'Party time!' and there was a flurry of activity as cameras and equipment were rolled aside, trays of food and bottles of wine miraculously appeared on the lawyers' tables, and a crate of beer was humped in by the brawnier members of the crew who proceeded to turn the judge's bench into a bar.

Over the noise, Shannon explained, 'We couldn't let you go without a farewell party.'

Rose laughed again, asking Devin, 'Did you know about this?'

'It was mentioned.' Shannon had told him yesterday of the plan, wondering if he'd find time to attend.

Craig appeared at Shannon's side and grinned at Rose. 'Come on,' he said, holding out his hand. 'I'll get you a drink.'

As they moved toward the impromptu bar, Craig's arm about Rose's shoulder, her face tilted to him, Devin stood looking after them.

He turned to Shannon, a peculiar expression on his face.

Trying not to speculate on what it meant, she asked him, 'How is your father? Have you seen him today?'

'He's on the mend. My mother is looking a lot less stressed too.'

Someone called Shannon, offering champagne, and she said, 'You are staying for the party? Help yourself, I have to organise getting the film to the lab for processing.'

By the time she'd done that and got herself a drink Devin was part of a group gathered about Rose, and Craig drifted to Shannon's side.

'She's gorgeous, isn't she?' he said wistfully, gazing at Rose.

'Yes.' Shannon suppressed a pang of envy.

Craig said, 'She invited me to go over and stay with her, even offered to recommend me for auditions, but

I don't know if I'm supposed to take it seriously. What do you think?'

'Rose seems a pretty genuine person,' Shannon said. 'I'd say go for it.'

'Thanks, hon.' He bent to give her a kiss.

Shannon slipped away from the party as soon as she decently could, hoping for a night's sleep. She was surprised when Devin arrived soon afterwards, while she was checking her shooting schedule for the following day, clad in pyjamas and sipping cocoa as she sat on a sofa.

She looked up and said, 'I didn't expect you back so soon.'

'There was no need to stay after you snuck away. Craig will look after Rose.'

'Yes, he will,' she said absently, returning to the pink paper in her hand. 'Are you taking her to the airport tomorrow, or should I lay on a car?'

'Whatever,' he said impatiently. 'Do you know she's talking of Craig joining her in L.A.?' he asked.

'Yes, he told me.'

'And…?'

'And I think he should take her up on it.'

'I…see,' he said slowly.

'What do you see?'

'You really don't care, do you? Were you ever at all in love with him?'

Shannon's head shot up. 'In love with…*Craig?* Of course not! I'm…' *I'm in love with you.* She swallowed the words. 'I can't imagine what gave you that idea.'

'You're very affectionate with each other. You understand each other, don't you, being in the same business? And he's very good-looking. When I first saw you together I was sure if he wasn't already involved with you, he'd like to be.'

'He's fond of me. I'm fond of him. We've been through some good and bad times in the business together. We're good friends.'

'I guess I'd forgotten how touchy-feely your friends are…your filming friends.'

True, there were a lot of hugs, kisses and casual endearments. The entertainment industry attracted outgoing personalities who openly showed their feelings, sometimes pretended to feelings they didn't have. Quite unlike Devin and his more restrained business contacts. 'I remember how you looked down your nose at them.'

'Not at all. They were such a colourful and exotic bunch, I felt like a particularly dull sparrow among a bevy of peacocks.'

'A *sparrow?*' A less apt description she could scarcely imagine. A hawk, more likely, whose shadow on the ground would send a bunch of peacocks screeching to the hills.

'I could see,' he said, 'that you might prefer someone who shared your creativity to a facts-and-figures man like me.'

Shannon shook her head. 'No.' And made bold by his confession, she added, 'What about Rose?'

'What about her?'

'You were very attentive to her.'

'I'd persuaded her to come here and be in your film.'

'Bribed her.'

'I paid her the going rate. She wouldn't have agreed if she hadn't liked the script. But I felt obliged to look out for her while she was here, and I wanted to save you the extra burden.'

He looked at her narrowly, then a faint smile lit his eyes, lifted his mouth. 'And she's a beautiful young woman,' he said. 'It didn't hurt a bit.'

'I'm sure it didn't,' she retorted with a snap, and stood up, clutching her papers to her chest. 'And I'm sure you'll enjoy seeing her off tomorrow.'

As she turned away Devin caught her arm, laughing, bringing her round to face him. She looked at him with fire in her eyes, her mouth stubborn, her body rigid.

'You're jealous,' he said, as matter-of-factly as if he were remarking that it was raining.

About to deny it, she saw how futile that was, and instead countered, 'Well, so are you!'

'Yes,' he conceded softly. 'And where does that leave us?'

Her mouth dried, her heart thumping. She didn't dare speak.

Devin said, 'You still have feelings for me…as I do for you, Shannon. Very deep feelings.'

Ages ago, it seemed, she'd been at least half convinced that he felt only a need to assert his will, to master her and punish her for leaving him. But they had come a long way in the last few weeks. This had nothing to do with revenge for past wrongs. 'What kind of feelings?' she asked. No matter how hard it was for him, she wanted it spelled out, no doubts, no concealment.

'Love,' he said simply, as if at last he could understand and meet her need for that reassurance. 'Passion. I never stopped loving you, Shannon. Even when I was furious and trying to convince myself you were shallow and selfish and not worth it, I couldn't help loving you, wanting you. And when I saw a remote, dim chance of bringing you back into my life—and keeping you away from Craig Sloane's bed—I jumped in with both feet—and nearly drowned in the process.'

'Drowned?'

'It was the wrong way to go about it, maybe fatal to renewing our marriage, but once I'd made the bargain I didn't dare let you back out. I did try to be different this time, more sensitive. I see you can't walk out and leave someone else to carry on when you're in the middle of a film. It's your vision that holds the thing together. And yet,' he said slowly, almost tentatively, 'you did exactly that when my father was taken ill.'

'I thought you might need me.'

Something flared then in the dark eyes. 'I did. Everyone else was looking to me to be the strong one, and you were just there for me. You'll never know how grateful I was for that.'

'Then I'm glad I did it.'

'So am I. It gave me a ray of hope, only I was too taken up with my father and the family to take advantage of it. And you've been pretty elusive.'

'We were running over schedule.'

He removed his hand from her arm. 'I'm releasing you from our contract, Shannon.' As her eyes widened, he said, 'Not the formal, written one. Your film is safe. But our unwritten agreement was unfair and unscrupulous, and I had no right to impose such conditions on you. So...' he looked up at the ceiling, drawing a deep breath before continuing '...you're free to go anytime you want.'

Blankly, she said, 'You're asking me to leave? Throwing me out?'

'No! I'm giving you a choice. And if you go I'm asking—*begging* you to let me see you again, give me a chance to show you that we could, maybe, have a real marriage again.'

He looked strained, and tense, as though holding himself under a tight rein.

Shannon wondered if this was a dream, a wish-fulfilment dream. Her voice low, and sounding as though it didn't belong to her, she said, 'I love you, Devin. I want to stay with you always.' She paused, bracing herself ready for heartbreak, yet knowing she had to do this. 'But I can't give up my career, even for you.'

'Have I hindered you in any way since you've been back?' he asked.

'No, and…before, I probably was a bit excessive,' she conceded. 'After my father died I was very frightened. It was bad enough when I lost my mother, but with him going too, having to relive that sense of abandonment brought home to me that even people who loved me couldn't be relied on to look after me.'

'That's what I wanted to do.'

'I know, and I couldn't let you. Deep down I was terrified that something would happen to take you away too. And the more you pushed me to let you care for me, the more determined I was to cling to my career and retain some independence, be responsible for myself.'

'Not financially,' he said. 'You know you would have been okay if I died. But emotionally?' he suggested slowly. 'To have a part of your life that didn't depend on someone you loved?'

Astonished at his unusual insight, she stared at him. 'I…yes, I suppose you're right. That's exactly it.' And ironically, because of her desperate determination to hold on to that, she had lost him.

'So everything I said only drove you further from me. You couldn't trust me to do what I promised. And that's why you rejected me.'

'I didn't mean to, I didn't realise what I was doing. Can you forgive me?'

'If you need forgiveness so do I.' He took her hands and looked down at them. 'I don't want to rush you into anything,' he said. 'You said you need to get this film out of the way before you start thinking about personal things. I can wait until you're ready.'

'Oh.' She peeped at him from under her lashes, deliberately provocative. 'I'm not sure I can.'

He lifted his eyes slowly, as if almost afraid of what he might see in hers.

What he saw was laughter and love, a hint of regret at what they'd missed during their estrangement, and the promise of passion. She tilted her head and looked back at him, bold and teasing.

'Shannon,' he said, the word very nearly inaudible, a groan welling straight from his heart. 'Oh, God, my darling, sweet, sweet Shannon.'

Then she was in his arms, and their mouths met with a hunger that burst into instant, all-consuming fire. He picked her up and carried her into his bedroom, fell onto the bed with her and kissed her again, a wild kiss of need and gladness and uninhibited sexuality.

He stopped long enough to tear off his clothes and help her with hardly less haste to get out of hers, and then they were mouth to eager mouth again, skin to skin, his hands finding softness and roundness, hers exploring muscle and tautly covered bone, the exciting contrast of smooth skin and wiry little curls of male hair on his body, the salty taste of him, and she breathed in a subtle masculine scent that made her dizzy with desire.

Nuzzling behind her ear, he murmured, 'You smell wonderful. You feel wonderful.' His hands told her so as they touched her cheek, her shoulder, waist, the curve of her hip. A strong thigh nudged hers apart and she arched into him, inviting his mouth to find her breasts, which it did, bringing her to a sighing, delicately poised brink of unnameable, unimaginable pleasure.

She moved to bring him closer, opened herself to him, and felt him filling her, warming her, giving himself utterly, and then the world burst into dazzling flame around them and consumed them both until they passed through the fire together and were cast into the cool washes of the night, still clinging to each other.

She was floating on a dark sea, safe and warm in Devin's arms where she belonged...where she had always belonged. Only somehow she'd been shipwrecked and thrown on some barren desert island without him. Until now...

'I'm home again,' she said at last.

He stirred against her, his arms tightening. 'So am I,' he said. 'Thank God. And you...Shannon, my lovely, loving wife. Back where we belong.'

EPILOGUE

THE premiere of *A Matter of Honour* was a glittering occasion.

The famous Rose Grady had flown in for a few days to attend, and she and her handsome co-star had just announced their engagement, and their plans to star in another film together. It was widely known that they had fallen for each other on the set of *Honour,* and interest in the sizzling onscreen affair was high. The media were jostling to get shots of the two of them, and clamouring for interviews.

Watching Rose and Craig pose for yet another photo after the show, Devin said in Shannon's ear, 'The stars get all the attention and the director's scarcely mentioned.'

'Neither are the rest of the crew,' she reminded him. 'The actors are our ambassadors. Anyway, I certainly don't want to attract too much attention looking like this!'

Devin looked down at her burgeoning figure and placed a hand over it. 'You look utterly, completely beautiful,' he said. 'I hope our little girl is going be just like you.'

This pregnancy had progressed normally but she was taking no chances. When she discovered she was expecting while *Honour* was in post-production, she'd announced she was taking some time off. She had enjoyed hunting for a house that was suitable both for entertaining and bringing up a family, and supervising the installation of a small theatre Devin had insisted she should have to view rushes with her crew in comfort.

She'd furnished a nursery and spent hours buying baby clothes, sometimes with her sister-in-law who was also pregnant. They joked that their babies might even share a birthday.

It had been fun, but when she and Devin moved to the new house and everything was in place Shannon had begun getting restless. Already she was planning her next film, a romantic thriller, with a starting date after the baby's birth.

'We'll get a good nanny,' Devin had promised, 'and she can bring the baby on location if necessary. Oh...I suppose a crying baby isn't a good idea on a film set.'

'No,' Shannon had agreed. 'But we could set up a special van or something. I don't want to be parted from my baby for days at a time.'

No doubt there would be hitches in their carefully laid plans but in filming the unexpected cropped up all the time and problems were made to be worked around. Devin was bending over backwards to support her career, and she was no longer deathly afraid of compromising it. The certainty of their love and commitment to each other had dissipated the tension.

'Are you up to this party?' he asked her as people began to move, heading toward the refreshments.

'I'm fine,' she said.

'I don't want to deprive you of your moment of glory, but you must look after yourself.'

Once that would have made her hackles rise. 'I hardly need to,' she teased him, 'when I've got you do it for me.'

'Do you mind?'

'No.' She smiled at him. 'I don't mind at all. And this is the last do like this we have to attend before the baby's born. After tonight I'm going to put my feet up.'

Her words were truer than she knew. April Rose Keynes made her presence decidedly felt the next morning, and by evening was already making her mark on the world and her parents' lives.

As Shannon cradled her new daughter in her arms Devin gazed down with a slightly stunned expression and took the baby's hand, watching in awe as April's tiny fingers wound about one of his. He looked up at Shannon and she saw tears in his eyes, for the very first time ever. 'I love you,' he said. 'I never knew how much until now. And I swear you'll never regret coming back to me.'

Shannon swallowed a lump in her throat. 'I know I won't,' she said. 'I'll never, never leave you again.'

'Don't you dare!' he said. 'It would kill me if you did.'

'It would kill me too,' she said. 'This time is for-ever.'

'Forever and beyond,' Devin agreed. And across their baby's downy head they sealed the vow with a kiss.

Modern Romance™
...seduction and
passion guaranteed

Tender Romance™
...love affairs that
last a lifetime

Sensual Romance™
...sassy, sexy and
seductive

Blaze
...sultry days and
steamy nights

Medical Romance™
...medical drama on
the pulse

Historical Romance™
...rich, vivid and
passionate

27 new titles every month.

*With all kinds of Romance for
every kind of mood...*

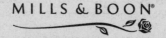
MILLS & BOON®

MB1

MILLS & BOON

Modern Romance™

THE HONEYMOON CONTRACT by Emma Darcy

A fantastic climax to the Kings of Australia trilogy! Matteo King is the last unmarried grandson of the Australian King dynasty – and he's determined to stay that way. Nicole Redman is shaken to the core by the sexual energy between them. What has Matt got in mind when he insists they discuss her contract – in the bedroom?

ETHAN'S TEMPTRESS BRIDE by Michelle Reid

A compelling story with intense emotion and hot, hot sensuality! Millionaire businessman Ethan Hayes told himself that Eve was a spoilt little rich girl, intent on bringing men to their knees. But when he found himself posing as her fiancé to calm her elderly Greek grandfather, suddenly it was all he could do to resist temptation…

HIS CONVENIENT MARRIAGE by Sara Craven

A warm, involving story with plenty of romantic tension! Miles Hunter had lived life on the edge, and he had the tortured pride to prove it. When he proposed marriage to Chessie, she knew he simply needed a social hostess. But Chessie owed Miles a great deal. Was he now expecting her to repay him – in his bed?

THE ITALIAN'S TROPHY MISTRESS by Diana Hamilton

Don't miss this gorgeous Latin hero! Cesare Andriotti always got what he wanted – and beautiful Bianca Jay was no exception. She hadn't been easy to win, but he had finally made her his mistress. Yet she intrigued him so much that he found himself proposing to her – only to be turned down!

On sale 2nd August 2002

Available at most branches of WH Smith, Tesco, Martins, Borders, Eason, Sainsbury's and most good paperback bookshops.

0702/01a

MILLS & BOON

Modern Romance™

RICCARDO'S SECRET CHILD by Cathy Williams

This book will remind you why you love Modern Romance – a classic! Riccardo Fabbrini was furious that his child had been kept from him. He blamed prim, pretty Julia Nash – and he intended to use his most powerful method of revenge, seduction! But with each kiss Riccardo's anger began to dissipate – to be replaced by something he'd never felt before...

THE VENETIAN MISTRESS by Lee Wilkinson

A wonderful story brought alive by vivid descriptions of Venice! A holiday romance is the last thing Nicola is looking for in Venice. But then she meets Dominic Loredan and they share a night of unbelievable passion. Dominic suggests Nicola become his mistress—dare she accept the Venetian's proposal?

THE PRINCE'S PLEASURE by Robyn Donald

A great royal story with breathless passion! Prince Luka of Dacia is a man with a lot to lose if his secret leaks out too early. He trusts nothing and no one – least of all his unexpected desire for Alexa Mytton. Torn between passion and privacy, Luka decides to keep her safely behind closed doors entirely for his pleasure...

SITTING PRETTY by Cheryl Anne Porter

Sex, lies and...family? Jayde Green should have been sitting pretty: house-sitting for millionaire Bradford Hale. But she hadn't expected to have to tell her parents a white lie in order to keep her job. And she certainly hadn't expected to fall for her gorgeous employer...

On sale 2nd August 2002

Available at most branches of WH Smith, Tesco, Martins, Borders, Eason, Sainsbury's and most good paperback bookshops.

0702/01b

M253

Women & Love

Three women...
looking for their perfect match

PENNY JORDAN

Published 19th July 2002

Available at most branches of WH Smith,
Tesco, Martins, Borders, Eason, Sainsbury's
and most good paperback bookshops.

0602/49/MB39a

MILLS & BOON®

heat *of the* night

LORI FOSTER

GINA WILKINS

VICKI LEWIS THOMPSON

3 SIZZLING SUMMER NOVELS IN ONE

On sale 17th May 2002

Available at most branches of WH Smith,
Tesco, Martins, Borders, Eason, Sainsbury's
and most good paperback bookshops.

Do you think you can write a Mills & Boon novel?

Then this is your chance!

We're looking for sensational new authors to write for the Modern Romance™ series!

Could you transport readers into a world of provocative, tantalizing romantic excitement? These compelling modern fantasies capture the drama and intensity of a powerful, sensual love affair. The stories portray spirited, independent heroines and irresistible heroes in international settings. The conflict between these characters should be balanced by a developing romance that may include explicit lovemaking.

What should you do next?

To submit a manuscript [complete manuscript 55,000 words]
OR
For more information on writing novels for Modern Romance™
Please write to :-
Editorial Department, Harlequin Mills & Boon Ltd, Eton House, 18-24 Paradise Road, Richmond, Surrey, TW9 1SR or visit our website at **www.millsandboon.co.uk**

Modern Romance...
"seduction and passion guaranteed"

Submissions to:
Harlequin Mills & Boon Editorial Department,
Eton House, 18-24 Paradise Road, Richmond, Surrey, TW9 1SR,
United Kingdom.

0602/WRITERS/MB40

2 FREE

books and a surprise gift!

We would like to take this opportunity to thank you for reading this Mills & Boon® book by offering you the chance to take TWO more specially selected titles from the Modern Romance™ series absolutely FREE! We're also making this offer to introduce you to the benefits of the Reader Service™—

- ★ FREE home delivery
- ★ FREE gifts and competitions
- ★ FREE monthly Newsletter
- ★ Exclusive Reader Service discount
- ★ Books available before they're in the shops

Accepting these FREE books and gift places you under no obligation to buy, you may cancel at any time, even after receiving your free shipment. Simply complete your details below and return the entire page to the address below. *You don't even need a stamp!*

YES! Please send me 2 free Modern Romance books and a surprise gift. I understand that unless you hear from me, I will receive 4 superb new titles every month for just £2.55 each, postage and packing free. I am under no obligation to purchase any books and may cancel my subscription at any time. The free books and gift will be mine to keep in any case.

P2ZEA

Ms/Mrs/Miss/Mr ....Initials................................
BLOCK CAPITALS PLEASE

Surname ....

Address ....

....

....Postcode ....

Send this whole page to:
UK: FREEPOST CN81, Croydon, CR9 3WZ
EIRE: PO Box 4546, Kilcock, County Kildare (stamp required)

Offer valid in UK and Eire only and not available to current Reader Service subscribers to this series. We reserve the right to refuse an application and applicants must be aged 18 years or over. Only one application per household. Terms and prices subject to change without notice. Offer expires 31st October 2002. As a result of this application, you may receive offers from other carefully selected companies. If you would prefer not to share in this opportunity please write to The Data Manager at the address above.

Mills & Boon® is a registered trademark owned by Harlequin Mills & Boon Limited.
Modern Romance™ is being used as a trademark.